THE GALLANT

STAR LEGEND BOOK 3

J.J. GREEN

"I drew this gallant head of war
And culled these fiery spirits from the world."

Shakespeare, *King John*

1

———

Wright was in deep shit, in more ways than one. His platoon had penetrated too deeply into an EAC-held district of Kingston, and now they were cut off from the rest of the Britannic Alliance forces. If they didn't fight their way out soon, they would all be killed.

Almost as bad, Brigadier Colbourn was furious with him.

He'd given Corporal Taylan Ellis a compassionate discharge without following proper protocol, and from the way the brigadier had reacted, he might as well have sold the BA's Caribbean assault plans to Dwyr Orr. *We are at war!* the brigadier had thundered. *You don't have the authority to give her a discharge.*

True.

Her connection with Arthur could make her vital to our plans.

Also true.

Now, his snap decision, taken out of sympathy for Ellis's plight, could mean his court martial, imprisonment, and even execution—after the Alliance finished retaking Jamaica.

An alarm blared, echoing from the surrounding buildings.

All around him in the factory where they'd taken refuge,

the Marines instinctively ducked. He'd guessed the same—it was an 'incoming' alarm. They were about to be bombed by their own side.

Great.

Kingston's power had been out ever since they'd landed a week ago, but pulse fire from enemy troops broke the overwhelming darkness of a cloudy night. The EAC hadn't moved on their position yet. They were keeping them pinned down, though, maybe waiting for reinforcements.

C-RAM kicked into life, spurting salvos of tracer slugs, trails of smoldering sparks. The juddering report of their firing shook his teeth and bones. Where the slugs destroyed the Alliance shells, explosions lit the sky like macabre fireworks.

This industrial sector of the city, where armament manufacturing plants abounded, was inevitably hotly contested. The Crusaders' automatic defense systems had been triggered. Would their troops be withdrawn? That would be the Alliance's hope, and, if the factory his platoon was sheltering in wasn't hit, they might make it out.

Boom!

The wall on the opposite side of the street exploded, spraying masonry into the air. A chunk of it crashed to the ground outside and shattered. Flames licked up in the bombed building, quickly growing brighter and taller.

Wright's comm sprang to life.

"SITREP, Major," said Lieutenant-General Carol, the officer coordinating the Royal Marines' role in the offensive.

"Still pinned down, sir."

Every attempt they'd made to leave had been met with heavy pulse fire. They were in a stinking situation, and that was before their own side started bombing them.

"Well, you'd better unpin yourselves," said the lieutenant-general. "The army are shelling the area."

"I'm aware of that, sir," Wright replied tersely.

Another missile made it through the C-RAM fire. The ground shuddered.

"They're aware of your presence," said Carol, "but securing that section of the city is vital. They held off as long as they could. The latest report says EAC presence south-west of you is minimal. Try to get out that way."

"Check." Wright had more to say but held his tongue. The previous report had stated the EAC had abandoned the industrial area. When they'd encountered resistance upon entering it, Carol had told him to press on. It was only rearguard action, he'd said. Then the enemy had closed in behind them.

He didn't place much faith in the reports.

"You're on your own, Major," said Carol. "Unfortunately, no one has any spare capacity to help you. When you get out, go to the Prime Minister's Palace."

"Understood, sir."

Carol closed the comm.

The Alliance's determination to win back Jamaica came easy when its military leaders were many kilometers distant. Carol was safely tucked away aboard *HMSS Gallant* in high Earth orbit. Wright wondered if he would be so bullish if he were here, hunkered down while death dropped from the sky.

Wright had no choice except to take the report at face value and attempt an exit to the south-west.

"We're leaving in two minutes," he told his platoon.

He ran to the relevant doorway to the outside, crouching low, dodging bench legs, half-built armaments, and production belts. A barrage of pulse fire was flashing at them. The EAC was redoubling its effort, predictably *not* trying to escape the shelling.

Propping his shoulder against the door jamb, he peeked out. They were in the center of a disaster zone. Abandoned vehicles, upturned dumpsters, and smashed-up food stalls littered the streets, along with the occasional corpse. The avenue leading south-west was a straight line. They would be able to travel fast down it, but they would also be easy targets for every EAC soldier watching from the surrounding buildings. It would be like running down the target end of a shooting range.

He gauged the intensity of enemy pulse fire coming from different locations and spied out what wreckage, recessed doorways, and overhangs would provide cover. Splitting the platoon into teams, he gave detailed orders. Sergeant Elphicke and Lance Corporal Patel would lead the teams that left first. The sergeant had been with him through many campaigns. Patel was new to her position, but she'd proven herself competent and trustworthy, if a little too eager.

He ordered all who could be spared from defending the factory to assemble at the exit.

Elphicke's group began laying down cover. Wright sped with his Marines toward an overturned truck. Their movement provoked a volley of shots from the enemy, despite the efforts of the covering team.

They made it to the truck.

Nestling his back against the truck's axle, he gave the signal. Patel's group burst out and sprinted for a dumpster farther down the street while Wright's sprayed fire at the hidden EAC troops.

It was time for Elphicke to leave. His team had the farthest to go—a bus shelter had miraculously survived the fighting unscathed. The metal shell wouldn't withstand solid rounds, but the enemy had stuck to pulse fire so far.

Wright gave the order, and the sergeant took his turn at being a moving target, along with his men and women. Patel's group helped provide cover, and the next team made ready to leave the factory.

And so the retreat began, each set of Marines leapfrogging another, gradually making their way down the street.

Meanwhile, the shelling had continued. The EAC's C-RAM was effective about three-quarters of the time. The final quarter of BA missiles were getting through, gradually turning the industrial district to burning rubble.

The last team left the factory and raced to the dumpster where Patel's group had briefly sheltered a few minutes before. Now it was Wright's turn.

"We're moving," he said to his team. "Stay tight and low."

Firing rearward at the enemy closing in on the now-deserted factory, he and his Marines left the truck and sprinted for the bus shelter, which was now little more than a smoking ruin.

Streams of tracer fire lanced across the sky. A missile screamed overhead and flew into an upper story window, exploding and blowing off the building's roof. Burning confetti showered down.

"Sir," came Patel's voice through his comm.

"What is it, Lance Corporal?"

"There's a barricade across the street. They've cut off our escape route."

He silently cursed. "How many hostiles?"

"Hard to tell. Not more than fifteen, I guess. We experienced less fire the farther we went, but now we're stuck."

So there had been some truth to the report. He synced with Patel's vidfeed. Blocking the street in front of her, turned side-on, were an armored personnel carrier, two jeeps, and an ice-cream van. All were piled high with debris from the streets, weighing them down. The ice-cream van stood in the center of the barricade, sporting the slogan *The Creamiest Ice in Jamaica* and, underneath, *Stop Me and Buy One.*

Emblazoned over the van's signage in massive letters was a single word of graffiti:

RESIST

The window was closed. There would be no iced treats for anyone today.

"Do you have any survi-drones left?"

"Uh...five, sir."

"Send them over the barricade."

Her vidfeed shifted as she complied.

The marble-sized drones activated and connected with his suit's system. Their visual and scan data amalgamated and played on his HUD, displaying a line of vehicles growing closer and then moving below. They reached the other side of the barricade. Eight EAC soldiers were near it and four or five more crouched in doorways. Then the display flashed red and cut out.

The Crusaders had an anti-drone device. It was to be expected. But the brief view he'd had of their setup was sufficient.

It was time for his team to leapfrog to their next position. They moved, attracting heavy fire. The troops to the rear were closer and becoming bolder. He thought about the barricade. If he delayed too long, his entire platoon would be caught against the barrier, sitting ducks. He made his decision. He would prefer to be there for the attempt, but he had no choice.

"Wait for Sergeant Elphicke to arrive, Patel, then try to break through. Keep me updated."

"Yes, sir."

He comm'd Elphicke.

He hoped Patel and the sergeant could do it.

To the rest of the platoon, he said, "Double time, Marines. We have business ahead."

Colbourn's wrath seemed a better alternative to what lay in store.

2

———

Taylan peered through binoculars over the rounded summit of a low hill in West BI. The grass beneath her was long, cold, and wet. She'd been lying in the same spot for hours. It was nearing midday, and she hadn't seen anything noteworthy. Though her waterproofs mostly protected her, rough blades poked in at her neck and ankles, chafing her exposed skin, and the chill from the ground had seeped into her bones.

From the numerous piles of crumbling sheep shit, she guessed the hill had once been used for grazing. But, judging by the length of the grass, no sheep had been here for a while. Had the Crusaders eaten them? Doing something so stupid and destructive would be right up their alley. They must have closed down the meat culturing factories or were they too dense to operate them. Sheep were for shearing, not eating.

Idiots.

In this case, the EAC's stupidity was to her advantage. The tall grass provided excellent cover while she spied on the orphanage.

The gray stain on the verdant landscape sat about a kilometer away, gouged from the bottom of the valley. A narrow road snaked toward it, ending at the gates. Within the perimeter fence sat ten pre-fabricated blocks with flat, asphalt roofs. The windows of nine of the blocks were curtain-less, and through them rows of child-sized bunk beds, tables, desks, and chairs could be seen. The tenth block appeared to be for the staff. Vertical blinds concealed the interior.

A high, chain link fence topped with razor wire enclosed the site, regularly patrolled by armed guards. Not a blade of grass nor any other green thing grew within the space. Outdoor play areas for the children were entirely absent.

What a place for kids to grow up.

It was more like a prison camp than an orphanage. But then, it wasn't really an orphanage because not all the kids were orphans. At least a few of the children's parents were probably still alive. Like her, their children had been lost or torn from them in the aftermath of the invasion, when the rush of refugees trying to leave the island had turned into a rout. Now most of the Britannic Isles' digital data had been destroyed by the EAC, parents had to rely on legwork and word-of-mouth to find their kids.

That was how she'd heard about the orphanage. Angharad, leader of the West BI Resistance, had put out feelers as soon as Taylan had told her of her predicament. Poor Angharad had died, but word had arrived of two kids who fit the description of her own at the orphanage.

Taylan rubbed her eyes with a finger and thumb. Nothing had stirred within the orphanage for ages. She placed the binoculars carefully on the ground, turned onto her back, and stared at the sky. Clouds were scudding past, dark and gravid with rain. A cool, humid wind was blowing, carrying the lingering odor of sheep as well as the faint scent of wildflowers.

It was good to be home.

It would be even better if her home wasn't infested with cockroaches.

Light raindrops began to fall, dampening her face. She rubbed her eyes again. Sleeping rough for two weeks had left her tired from the moment she woke up. And she was hungry. The West BI Resistance had given her rations along with the binoculars and other equipment she felt quite guilty accepting, considering such items were in short supply, but her food had nearly run out.

She had to find Kayla and Patrin soon before she was forced to steal to survive. In the current situation she had no ethical qualms about stealing, but if she was caught she would end up dead, sooner or later. Preferably sooner. Dwyr Orr knew who had shot her in Jamaica, and now she was after her blood. The Dwyr would not dispense death quickly to Taylan Ellis.

The rain grew heavier.

She'd been watching the orphanage for three days without a glimpse of either of her children. In all her hours of scrutiny, she'd only seen the captive kids thirty or forty minutes in total. They rarely left their dorms, and when they did it was only in order to walk to another block. Dressed in a uniform of dark jacket and pants, the kids walked with their heads bowed.

What did they do all day?

Undergo indoctrination, Taylan answered herself. Even Crusaders weren't sufficiently depraved to murder children. Instead, they lied to them and misled them, twisting their minds, turning them into true believers who forgot about their parents and their past lives.

Had Kayla and Patrin already forgotten about her?

She drew in a deep breath.

A tinny sound came to her ears, like the distant noise of a door opening. She spun onto her front. The binoculars contained a directional mic, and when she'd put them down, she'd pointed them at the orphanage.

One of the doors in the staff block was ajar, and a man and a woman were about to descend the wooden steps.

Taylan centered the mic on them.

"I hope my transfer comes through soon," said the man. "I'm sick of this place. I hate teaching those whiny brats."

The woman quietly *shushed* him. They didn't speak again until they were several meters distant from the block.

"You should be more careful," she said. "What if someone heard you? You know what they're like."

"Yeah, and that's another reason I want a transfer. They're watching us as much as we're watching the kids."

"They have to be sure we're teaching them the right stuff in the right way. It's confusing for children to go from one system of beliefs and thoughts to another. They're being careful we don't slip up."

"Stop making excuses for them. You're as bad as they are."

"I just understand their point of view."

"I'm glad *someone* does," the man said sarcastically.

They had nearly reached another block. Taylan chewed her lip. The pair's conversation was useless to her. Couldn't they at least mention a couple of names? Did they even know the kids' names? Maybe they gave them new ones.

As the couple reached a corner, the man grabbed the woman's elbow and pulled her around it, out of general sight. He said something, but the mic didn't pick it up. Taylan cursed and quickly adjusted it. Even so, after re-focusing it on the couple, she only barely made out what was said next.

"I don't see what there is to be afraid of," the woman said.

"You know as well as I do we're a prime target for insurgents. People will do a lot to get their kids back."

"Then it's fortunate for us all their parents are dead."

"Don't be naive. Plenty of them are still hiding out in the hills."

"All right, maybe there are a few. But the patrols will get them all eventually. No one would dare to attack us."

Patrols?

"I'm not so sure. The sooner I get out of this place the better."

"Good for you. Now let's go in, or they'll be wondering where we've got to."

Taylan had been careful since leaving the Resistance hideout, always traveling at night and keeping out of sight. She hadn't seen anyone else in the lonely landscape, but her eavesdropping had confirmed the EAC did have people scouring the hills for natives they hadn't managed to kill yet.

She'd been lucky so far. It was even more reason to locate her kids and get them to safety quickly.

Lifting the binoculars, she scanned the hills on the other side of the valley. The high, grassy mounds were empty of life except for birds and the odd rabbit. In her current position it was harder to see what was happening on her side, but she appeared to be alone.

The view trembled, and she realized she was shivering.

It was time to move around a bit and get her circulation going.

After another glance at the landscape, she rose to a crouch and then began to edge backward down the slope. When she was lower than her own height to the ridge, she rose to her feet but remained bent down low as she made her way toward the wood where she'd spent the last two nights.

The hill ran down to a stone wall, one of many turning the fields into a giant chessboard. The wood covered the low ground too wet for grazing and straggled up the hills on each side. She'd stashed her belongings within the roots of a willow.

She reached the outer trees. Halting, she looked behind her

and to each side. Nothing moved in the landscape except crows riding the wind. She waded through the trackless bracken until she reached her campsite. Her sleeping bag and backpack hadn't changed position since she'd left them.

Pulling a ration bar from her pack, she sat down to eat it.

Regrets over her recent past ran through her head. Joining the Marines had been a terrible mistake. How could she have given up looking for her kids so easily? But she'd been messed up, blaming herself for giving Kayla and Patrin over to someone else's care. It was no wonder she'd made only one friend and many enemies among her fellow Marines. They hadn't liked her beating them all the time in Basic, but her attitude had sucked too.

Never mind.

She couldn't take back the past, and at least now she was finally back on track.

She popped the last of the bar into her mouth. It was time to head back up the slope and continue her vigil, but tiredness dogged her. It probably wouldn't hurt to take a nap. The kids in the orphanage would all be eating lunch.

She lay down on the leaf mold and pulled her sleeping bag over her rather than climbing into it. That way, she wouldn't get too comfortable and sleep too long.

An unknown amount of time later, a loud rustling woke her.

Her muscles rigid, she listened. It sounded like two or three people striding through the undergrowth. The sound of their passage was accompanied by whacks, as if they were hacking at vegetation with knives or sticks.

The noises were growing louder.

She opened her eyes. The dappled light had grown soft. She guessed she must have slept a couple of hours. About twenty meters away, three figures strode through the waist-height bracken, heading toward her. Very slowly, she slid out from under her sleeping bag.

"Something moved over there!" a voice yelled. "Can you see it?"

Shit!

Taylan bolted.

3

———————

They were trapped.

Two bodies lay on the asphalt in front of the barricade. Another Marine was injured—mortally according to his stats. Wright had called a halt to the attack as soon as he'd arrived at the barrier and seen how hopeless it was. Though they outnumbered the troops on the other side, they couldn't attempt to move the vehicles or climb over them without exposing themselves to enemy fire. And he had nothing except his men and women to throw at the problem. Weapons-wise, they were down to pulse rifles only. With nothing heavier, they were never going to break through the blockade, and they were barely holding off the EAC approaching from the rear.

Lieutenant-General Carol had made it clear no one could be spared to come to their rescue. They had to make it out by themselves or not at all. Wright had been in tight spots before, but none as tight as this.

Recessed shop doorways and abandoned vehicles were providing the bare minimum of cover for now. At least the shelling had stopped. The cessation in friendly fire was buying his platoon some respite, but it would also give their attackers more freedom to finish them off.

The only possible escape lay in entering the buildings and hoping to find alternative exits leading into surrounding alleys and streets. One of the buildings was a large, well-known department store. It had to have a rear entrance for deliveries. But that could mean splitting up, with every Marine for themselves, in an area alive with hostiles. It was likely they would be rounded up one by one, and everyone knew the EAC took no prisoners. He filed the option in the back of his mind to be used as a last resort. If there was a way they could stick together...

Pulse fire flashed in the darkness behind. The second half of the trap was closing.

His gaze fell upon a manhole cover.

Why try to go through the barricade when they could go under it?

"Sergeant Elphicke, I want you to go down into the sewer and try to find a route out of this mess. Take three Marines with you." Wright shared his vidfeed so the sergeant could see what he meant. Strictly speaking, the man would be going *into* a mess.

A pause.

"Roger wilco."

Wright ordered the rest of the platoon to lay down cover, forward and to the rear.

The sewer would follow the street. All Elphicke had to do was find a place where it was safe to leave it. Wright watched as he ran for the manhole, hefted it to one side, and slipped into the hole, quickly followed by his team.

Enemy fire from behind was intensifying. The EAC on the far side of the barricade seemed content to let their buddies take the majority of the risk, shooting only sporadically from their secure position. Wright diverted five Marines to the rear defense. He'd lost contact with Elphicke as soon as he'd disappeared underground. He wouldn't see him or his team again on his HUD until they surfaced.

One of the dots that signified the members of his platoon turned blue. It was the man who had been wounded in the assault on the barricade.

Wright silently cursed. This was like death by a thousand cuts.

A minute dragged past.

He decided to update Carol.

After giving his brief report, he asked, "What's happening in the rest of the city, sir?"

"You're still on your own, I'm afraid, Major. But hopefully your plan will succeed. Remember, the Prime Minister's Palace." Carol cut the comm.

The Prime Minister's Palace sounded like a far-off dream. What had happened to Elphicke?

A Marine leapt from the open manhole, quickly followed by another.

"EAC on our tails!" the first to emerge yelled. He grabbed the cover and thrust it over the hole.

"Wait!" said Wright. "What about Elphicke?"

"Dead, sir."

The other Marine was dragging a dumpster toward the manhole.

"Elphicke and Moss," the man added. "We were spotted as soon as we climbed out."

The second Marine had pulled the heavy dumpster on top of the cover.

A sudden grief hit Wright. He'd known Elphicke for years. They hadn't been close, but... He pushed his feelings aside. There would be time to think about Elphicke later.

His plan had failed and cost two lives, and he'd given the EAC another avenue of attack: from below.

From below.

If they couldn't go under the street...

He looked upward.

The buildings all adjoined one another. Could they simply cross from one roof to the next? Now the shelling had stopped, the idea wasn't completely crazy.

Lance Corporal Patel was sheltering in the recessed doorway of the department store. Wright explained his idea, planning on sending her to scout out the route to the roof and report whether an escape that way was feasible. Then he changed his mind. He'd already lost one good officer. This time, he would go along and comm the rest of the platoon to follow when he knew it was safe.

"Don't go in yet," he said. "I'm coming with you."

After comming the Marines to continue to defend against the rearward attack and await further orders, he dashed across the street to the opposite side.

"Why's your visor open?" he asked Patel when he saw her young face.

"I took a hit on it, sir. Couldn't see a thing."

Wright was glad he'd picked her to help him find an exit over the rooftop. Operating without the benefit of a HUD was like fighting with one hand behind your back.

"Come with me," he said to her and the two Marines sheltering with her, Bates and Snowdon.

The store's doors were locked but the glass had been smashed by looters. He stepped over the door frame and into the shadowy interior. Empty shop shelves filled most of the space and discarded, broken goods covered the floor—useless things, like bottles of perfume, cosmetics, costume jewelry, and swimwear.

They ran for the escalator and bounded up the frozen steps. A turn, and another set of escalators. Another turn, and another run upward.

Five more floors later, they came to the final of the escalators, which ended in an amusement center. The machines were silent and dark. The four Marines' helmet lights swept the place as each looked for a route onto the roof.

"I think I see an exit sign," said Patel. She set off across the room quickly, weaving between the sim globes and holo cubicles.

"Slow down, Lance Corporal," said Wright. "I don't want us to get sep—"

"It's here, sir!" she exclaimed.

"Patel!" yelled Wright. "Wait!" He dashed to catch up to her.

At the same time, there was a clunk, like the sound of a heavy bar being pressed down, followed by the creak of hinges.

"Patel!"

Pulse fire spurted through the open door.

Wright reached the lance corporal just in time to catch her in his arms as she fell backward. She'd been hit in the face through her open visor. He turned his head away from the sight. Another pulse bolt flew through the door, hitting Patel in the stomach. Her armor blackened and smoked, but she was already dead anyway.

Bates threw himself at the door and slammed it shut. It locked automatically, only opening from the inside.

"Sir," said Snowdon, "we have to get out of here."

Wright realized he'd frozen. "Yes...I..."

He couldn't seem to let go of Patel.

"We'll have to leave her, Major," said Bates.

The two Marines looked at each other. Snowdon gently pulled Patel out of Wright's arms and laid her down.

"Sir," said Bates sharply. "Do we go back down to the street?"

The door resounded as something struck it.

"Yes," said Wright, his voice sounding like a stranger's. "Back down to the street."

"Check," Snowdon said. "Let's go."

His words triggered Wright into action. Bates leading, they ran for the head of the escalator and began bounding down it.

Wright tried to think of something else to try when they reached the street, but his mind was playing a two-second vid on a loop: a door opening, pulse fire, Patel sinking into his arms, her ruined face.

4

———

Taylan's feet thudded through the long grass. Her panting and the whistle of the wind were loud in her ears. Her lungs, heart, and muscles seemed to scream at her, begging her to stop, but she couldn't.

Stopping was certain death.

At first, she'd run straight, putting as much distance between herself and the Crusaders as she could, hoping to crest a hill and dip out of sight before they emerged from the wood. Then a pulse round had hit the ground beside her, flaming the vegetation. So she'd begun to zigzag randomly, presenting a harder target.

All the while, the slope she was racing up appeared never-ending. She longed to reach the top, even though, realistically, it was unlikely she would escape then. But the respite of being temporarily out of sight would be welcome.

Another round hit the ground, incinerating the exact spot where her foot had been a split second earlier.

She realized she was running faster for the same amount of effort. The slope was leveling off. She was near the top of the hill. She risked a glimpse of what was happening behind her.

Three figures were visible. Two men and a woman were toiling up the rise. Only one was armed.

Ahead of her the landscape opened out into wide pasture on the farther side of the hill.

Not a road, wall, hedgerow, or other hiding place was in sight.

Her thumping heart plummeted into her stomach. Her only chance of survival was to outrun her pursuers, and avoid being shot. If only she could magic herself to the size of a rabbit and disappear down a hole.

Where was Merlin when you needed him?

Taking advantage of the downward slope, she opened out her stride. The rough grass flew past beneath her, only the balls of her feet making contact with the ground. Briefly, she thought of everything she'd left behind: Binoculars, sleeping bag, food, water bottle—everything the West BI Resistance had loaned her. If she managed to get away, she would have little more than the clothes she wore. She would have to give up searching for Kayla and Patrin, temporarily at least.

Damn the Crusaders!

Damn them for making her lose her children.

Damn them for all the people they'd killed.

A sudden agony erupted on the back of her right thigh and she caught a whiff of an acrid scent—the odor of her own seared flesh.

She'd been hit.

The ground and sky became a whirling, spinning confusion. Her hips and shoulders were buffeted by bumps and grass whipped her face over and over as she rolled down the slope.

When she stopped, with no place to crawl to and hide, her pursuers would catch up to her in seconds.

And then what?

She remembered Wilson, horrifically tortured by Dwyr Orr,

displayed for all to see at the ceremony intended to launch the invasion of Ireland.

A quick death would be better.

She was slowing down. She snatched at tussocks. They tore out of her hands, but she slowed herself a little more. Then she held onto one tussock so tightly her motion didn't jerk it from her hand.

She stopped.

Her right leg was a throbbing mess of pain, utterly useless. Even if she hadn't been surrounded by open countryside, she couldn't have got away.

Grimly, she awaited her hunters.

One of the men was the first to reach her. Breathless, he slid to a halt on his knees and turned excitedly to his companions. "She's here! You winged her, Stefan."

He was wearing the Crusaders' strange garb, simple clothes that looked hand woven and hand sewn.

Taylan seized the man's shoulder, yanking it to pull herself closer. In one smooth movement, she pulled out her knife and thrust it under his ribs. She gave it a twist to make sure she cut something vital and then jerked the blade free. Blood gushed out, drowning her wrist. His mouth formed an O of surprise as she pushed him down and faced her two remaining attackers.

They were not so foolhardy. The man aimed the rifle at her as he trotted down the slope. The woman ran a short distance behind him, her white-faced gaze on the expiring body at Taylan's side. Both halted ten paces from her.

"Drop the knife," the Crusader with the rifle ordered.

She hesitated.

A fast, certain death or agonizing torture along with a tiny chance of escape?

She tossed the knife. It sank blade downward into the soft soil.

Should she tell them her name? It would guarantee her

survival in the short term, but she still wasn't sure if she wanted to survive. Killing the first of her pursuers to reach her had been almost a reflex action.

Before she could say anything, the man said to the woman, "Is it her? What do you think?"

Had they seen a picture of her? Had the Dwyr Orr managed to find one? Perhaps she'd created an image in the same way she'd created holos of Kayla and Patrin, based on Wilson's memories of her vids.

Except that hadn't been the Dwyr's work. Arthur had said another person was responsible—Morgan le Fay.

"Could be," said the woman. "She fits the description."

The man glanced at the figure on the ground. "And she's definitely a killer."

The man she'd stabbed breathed his last.

"I'll hold the rifle while you tie her up," the woman said.

"Huh." The man gave her a knowing, sidelong glance.

Taylan couldn't blame her for her reluctance. *She* wouldn't want to come near herself either.

In answer to his companion's offer, the man lifted the rifle strap over his head and shoved the weapon into her hands.

Approaching Taylan, he said, "No sudden moves, all right?" He was pulling a rope from his pocket.

She didn't answer.

She never made promises she couldn't keep.

"Maybe we should just kill her," blurted the woman.

"The Dwyr wants her alive, if it *is* her."

"We could say it was an accident. She fought back, and—"

"We'll get a better reward if she's alive," the man insisted.

He was within two paces of Taylan. They were having a staring competition she was confident she would win.

"Just keep the rifle on her."

The woman shifted on the spot, adjusting her aim.

"Stand up."

Her thigh screaming its protest, she got to her feet, carefully adjusting her position to take account of her wound.

"Arms behind your back," said the man.

Without her gaze leaving his, she obeyed.

"That's it," said the man, relieved. "No need to make this harder than it has to be."

He'd reached her.

"I'm glad we agree," she said, stooping to take her other knife from her boot.

She grabbed the man's hair, pushed the knife tip into the dip between his windpipe and neck muscle, and jerked him in front of her.

"Lose the gun," she ordered.

The woman's gaze flicked from the blade to Taylan and then to the man's eyes.

One hand full of his hair and her other around the knife hilt, Taylan urged him forward and moved with him. As her right leg was forced to bear some of her weight, she ground her teeth.

"Wh-what should I do?" the woman asked.

"Whatever you do," replied the man, "don't shoot."

"Should I—"

"*Lose it!*" Taylan ordered.

Another shove of the trembling man, another hop.

The woman's expression hardened. She lifted the rifle higher and squinted through the viewfinder, probably imagining Taylan was so close now she could take her out without harming the man.

Wrong.

She jabbed the knife. In and out. Blood gushed from his neck. Giving him a final, hefty push, she sent his dying body toward the female Crusader.

Her eyes popping in horror, the woman stumbled backward.

Taylan sprang forward on her good leg, knocked aside the rifle muzzle, and threw herself on the woman. Another jab of the knife, and the final Crusader's lifeblood began spurting freely from her neck through clasping fingers.

The pain of her wound overwhelming her, Taylan collapsed. She waited. When the waves receded a little, she lifted her head. A quick survey of the landscape told her she was alone with the three bodies. But things might not stay the same for long. The dead Crusaders could be members of a larger group.

On the plus side...she pulled the blood-stained rifle away from the dead woman...she was armed. But her leg was bad, and she had nothing more than a simple first-aid kit stashed in her backpack a mile or more away in the wood. She crawled, favoring her good leg, to the knife she'd tossed away. After wiping both her blades clean on the grass, she replaced them in their sheaths.

It was time to start moving.

5

———

How old had Patel been? Twenty? Twenty-one?

Wright guessed the EAC must have spotted his team entering the department store and anticipated where they were going. Patel hadn't stood a chance. If only she'd waited, been more cautious, but she was young, too young. He should have taken her over-eagerness into consideration and left her in the street with the others. It was his fault she'd died.

Elphicke had been married with a family at home in Australia.

Had he put too much responsibility on Elphicke by asking him to find an underground escape route? Maybe he should have led the attempt himself.

Maybe *he* should be dead, not his sergeant.

Crouching behind a dumpster, Wright wondered what to tell his platoon. He couldn't lie and tell them reinforcements were on their way, that all they had to do was hold out until their rescuers arrived. Unless...

Opening a comm, he asked Lieutenant-General Carol, 'Sir, are any BA forces near our current position?'

Seconds passed as he waited for an answer.

'Negative, Major. SITREP.'

Wright gave his report.

There was a pause before Carol replied, "I'm sorry, Major. If there was anything I could do…"

"I understand, sir." He cut the comm.

Gritting his teeth, Wright peeked out from the dumpster he was using as cover. The EAC approaching from the rear had become bolder, and sniper fire from windows beyond the barricade was scoring plenty of near misses. It was only a matter of minutes before they were overwhelmed. After a short analysis of the facts, he told his surviving Marines their next move: an all-out offensive on the barricade. It was going to be their final and only chance of survival.

Swinging out from his cover, he joined the assault. The Marines were running at full tilt toward the barrier. Pulse fire exploded from windows and the gaps between the vehicles. A stray bolt destroyed the facade of the ice-cream truck so all it read was *Jamaica* and *Stop*.

Someone was climbing up the side of a personnel carrier. As soon as he reached the top, a flash erupted on his breastplate and he crashed to the ground. But another Marine was also climbing. As he clawed his way onto the roof, he was already firing. A third man joined him.

A group had their shoulders against a jeep and were trying to push it out of the way, but distorted steel beams from destroyed buildings ran through it. The small gap they created was soon alive with pulse bolts.

Wright scaled the other jeep one-handed, holding his rifle in the other. A chunk of masonry came loose and tumbled to the ground, nearly taking him with it. As he reached the top, he came face to face with a Crusader. The muzzle of his rifle happened to be pointing in the right direction. Reflexively, his finger closed on the trigger and the pulse exploded on the Crusader's visor. He disappeared.

One for Patel.

Scorching heat emanated from his neck and shoulder. He'd been hit. He looked up and caught a glimpse of a figure in a blown-out window. Aiming, he fired. The pain became too great, and the hand he was holding on with opened involuntarily. He fell backward onto pavement.

Despite the protection of his armor, the impact knocked the breath out of him.

He struggled to suck air in.

Above him, flashes lit the sky.

He briefly thought the C-RAM had started up, but its staccato report was absent. The flashes were pulse fire, and...he managed to lift his head a little...they were coming from beyond the barricade.

The EAC were fighting on ground they held?

He turned onto his front and staggered to his feet. The number of downed Marines had increased, but the overall number was fewer. Some had made it over the barricade. Perhaps that was the source of the pulse fire he could see. But it seemed too much for his platoon to account for it. He could barely move his left arm, but he decided to have another go at getting over the barricade.

Before he could clamber onto the jeep, however, someone began pulling down the debris piled on top of it. Someone on the *other* side.

The Crusader snipers were still firing, but they were firing at *their* side of the street. As Wright watched, the sniper fire lessened.

In another ten minutes, it was all over.

The barricade was torn down, Wright's platoon helping. He watched, confused, the pain from his wound increasing as his adrenaline ebbed.

The Crusaders had been neutralized by an unexpected, unknown ally.

A mound of debris crashed to the ground and a jeep shifted position, opening up a gap.

"Major," someone comm'd him. A Marine beckoned toward the break in the barricade.

The obstacle that had thwarted him for... how long? It had probably been no more than twenty or thirty minutes, though he felt like hours had passed. The obstacle had finally been overcome. But he didn't know how. Maybe Carol had managed to organize a relief force after all.

The windows in the buildings on the far side of the barrier were black and empty. The snipers were gone, probably dead. The cultists usually preferred to die rather than fall into enemy hands.

He stepped through the gap.

A man approached him, dressed in armor of a style Wright hadn't seen for a decade and carrying a similarly outdated rifle. The answer to his confusion popped into his mind.

It was the Resistance. The Jamaican Resistance had come to their rescue.

Wright raised his visor and held out his hand. "I can't thank you enough."

The man's hand remained by his side. He replied grimly in a Jamaican accent, "We don't want your thanks. We want you to leave our country. You aren't welcome here."

6

———

The fruit seller had a securibot. If you didn't approach the stall from the front, like an honest, regular customer, it would shoot you with a laser beam. The beam could penetrate cloth and burn skin. Kala knew this for a fact. She had the scars to prove it.

But she was hungry.

The fruit stall was one of the few places in the market that displayed its wares within easy grabbing distance. Things had been tough lately, even for people who had jobs and homes—an increasingly small minority—and the stallholder probably wanted to tempt customers to part with the meager contents of their bank accounts. When food was a luxury, fruit came last on shopping lists.

Kala wasn't fussy about what she stole to fill her belly, providing the securibot didn't get her.

The device hung from the rear of the stall, a metal sphere dotted with small, flat lenses and spikes that shot laser rays. The vendor was standing with his back to her, busy serving customers from the front. Her gaze moved from the securibot to a display of peaches, plump, pink, perfectly ripe.

Her stomach growled.

From among the general chattering from the shoppers, two voices grew louder. Too late, Kala looked up. She was just in time to see a heavy-set woman in a dark overcoat before the woman collided with her. Kala's small body bounced off the large-framed lady and as she fell she cracked her knee on the curb. The impact tore her skin open. Blood dribbled from the cut. The woman had stumbled only a little, but she cursed and berated Kala for being 'in the way' though of course it was her own fault. She hadn't been looking where she was going. She'd been too deep in conversation with her tall, wispy-haired friend.

Kala lifted her upper lip in a snarl and spat into the muddy gutter. The heavy woman's friend grabbed her elbow and guided her away, complaining how the street rats were becoming a real problem nowadays. Kala pulled the sleeve of her dirty sweater over the heel of her hand and dabbed at her knee. The graze wasn't too bad, but dirt from the gutter had got into it. She would have to wash it and ask Jon the Apothecary for something to smear on it to stop an infection. He would help her. He was a soft touch.

She returned her attention to the securibot.

Was it watching her back? Probably. It would be programmed to detect suspicious behavior, and her loitering would have alerted it. But it wouldn't fire unless she got too close.

Her knee ached. Blood had broken out afresh and was cutting channels through the mud on her legs. Her stomach hurt too.

Ah, mud.

She looked from the patch of mud where she'd fallen to the glass camera lenses on the bot. Squatting down, she began to scoop up the gloopy dirt. If she had a good aim, she could—

"Kala, can you hear me?"

She paused and looked up and around. Shoppers passed by, uninterested in the little girl playing in the mud. Concluding she must be mistaken, that she'd misheard a snatch of conversation, she dipped her hands into the mud again.

"Kala, it's Morgan. If you can hear me, try saying something in reply."

She shot up. The mud oozed from between her fingers and dripped onto the wet pavement. *Morgan?* Who the hell was Morgan? She looked around again. No one was paying any attention to her.

Kala's head began to ache. The pain started behind her eyes but quickly spread until it felt like someone had fastened her skull in a vise and was tightening it. She put her filthy hands to her temples and squeezed her eyes closed, trying to shut out the agony, but it only increased. Her brain was a fireball, burning out through her orbits.

She screamed.

She opened her eyes upon darkness. The faintest of vibrations and quietest of hums nibbled at the edge of her consciousness. Where was the street market, the securibot, and the peaches? Where was the mud?

And Jon. There was something significant she'd forgotten about Jon.

The pain was receding. She heard herself panting, but her breaths were growing longer and deeper. Understanding flowed into her mind, and the years between her childhood and now came flooding back. She was the leader of the Earth Awareness Crusade and she was aboard the flagship of her space fleet, the *Belladonna*. Morgan was here too—the hated Morgan le Fay she'd unwittingly released from captivity—as well as Perran. She'd retreated to space, specifically Earth-Sun Lagrange 5 after the terrifying attempt on her life at the ceremony to launch the invasion of Ireland.

As she sat up, her cabin lights came on. Wincing, she said, "Lights, dim."

She rubbed her temples. The threads of her dream were fading, but she found herself wishing Jon was aboard the ship. He might be able to give her something to help with the...

In her mind's eye, she saw an image: a pair of feet, one bare, old and wrinkled, and one stuffed into a slipper, swinging in the breeze below a castle window. She shook her head, trying to shake away the painful picture.

It was not her fault.

If Jon had decided to take exception to her methods for governing her people, that was up to him. She wasn't responsible for his choices. It was not her problem that he hadn't understood. Yet, no matter what she told herself, the dull ache she'd felt since his suicide would not abate. Her hurt flashed into anger.

Why had he done this to her? He must have known how taking his own life would affect her. She'd lost the only remaining contact with her past, the only person who knew her before she rose to power. The only person she could truly trust. Her only friend.

He must have wanted her to blame herself, to make her look again at what she was doing with her life. Well, he wasn't going to reach out from beyond the grave and get his way. She refused to give him another thought.

Nevertheless, fury stalked her while she got out of bed and pulled on her robe. After knotting the ties, she stalked stiffly out into the passageway.

Morgan's cabin was one minute's walk away, but Kala reached it in half the time. When the door didn't open immediately, she used her security override and stormed inside.

"What the hell was that?" she demanded.

Morgan was wearing a nightdress made of a fine, clinging material. She sat bent over an interface embedded into a desk.

Through the open doorway to the bedroom, Kala could see a man sleeping in her bed under ruffled, luxurious sheets, naked from the waist up.

She scowled. Didn't Morgan understand it was a bad idea to sleep with the crew? She was inviting insubordination, friction, even mutiny.

Morgan hadn't lifted her gaze from the interface. "I thought you wanted to practice," she replied mildly. "You *said* you wanted to practice."

"Not while I was asleep! You knew I was asleep and dreaming, didn't you!" It was an accusation, not a question.

Her shoulders rising slightly in a shrug, Morgan replied, "I'm not sure what difference it makes."

"It makes *all* the difference. Arghh!" Kala pressed the heels of her hands into her eyes and sat on a sofa. "God, my head hurts. Why didn't you tell me it would be so painful?"

Another shrug. "I'm not sure how I could be expected to know that. I don't make a habit of teaching humans telepathy."

When she finally looked at Kala, Morgan's eyes were narrowed and her features full of spite and peevishness. "If you don't want to learn, tell me now. I won't tolerate your complaints when I'm trying to be helpful. Remember, *you* asked *me* to do this, not the other way around."

Kala clenched her teeth and looked down. She had *so much* to say in reply, but she couldn't, she mustn't. Instead, she nursed her aching head. Moving to the comm panel next to the door, she requested medication from the sick bay. Folding her arms over her chest, she said, "I suppose now I'm awake and here, it's a good time to discuss my next move to ensure my safety."

Morgan's gaze had returned to her interface.

"I received a report that one of my search patrols in West BI had gone missing," Kala pushed on. "They were found a day later, all murdered. They'd died from knife wounds, which makes me think it wasn't an organized BI Resistance attack.

They're better armed than that, unfortunately. I think Taylan Ellis might have killed them. We know she didn't arrive in Ireland with the rest of the BA party."

"She has remained in West BI to look for her children," Morgan murmured. "That's obvious." She straightened up and looked Kala in the eyes. "She's dangerous, but she shouldn't be your focus. She isn't your greatest threat. She's a secondary character."

"Character? You make it sound like we're in a vid."

"As I've told you many times," Morgan went on, "Arthur is the one you must focus on." Softly, she added, "And I must focus on *my* enemy."

Who was her enemy?

Kala wasn't sure she dared to ask. "But Taylan Ellis is the one who hurt me. I want her dead."

"If Arthur had reached you with Excalibur," said Morgan, "there wouldn't have been a thing I could have done to stop him killing you."

Kala shivered and ran her hands up and down her upper arms. "I should never have held the ceremony. It was far too risky."

"Hiding away isn't the answer. Your people want and need to see you. They must see you're unafraid before they'll follow you. Arthur was never afraid."

"When he was king?"

"Then, and now."

"It's easy to be fearless when you're impervious to harm."

Morgan lifted an eyebrow. "And easy to be scared when you aren't. But Arthur isn't completely invulnerable. It would have been better if you'd managed to kill him before the Alliance found him."

"The ship that picked Arthur up in Ireland took him to the *Gallant*," said Kala. "He must still be aboard it. If I can destroy the ship, he'll die."

In the bedroom, Morgan's evening entertainment was waking up. He rolled onto his back and stretched his arms out wide. When he sat up, Kala vaguely placed him as one of the cooks. Her nose wrinkling, she yelled, "You! Get out!"

Morgan chuckled again but didn't object.

The man instantly recognized his mistress's voice and quickly pulled on his pants. Grabbing his shirt and shoes, he moved quickly out of the bedroom. Kala drew back with distaste as he passed her.

Pain lanced her head again, and she bit back a cry. Cradling her forehead, she winced as she looked at Morgan, expecting she was sending to her once more. But the voice that entered her mind wasn't a woman's.

"Mummy," Perran said, "Mummy, are you awake? Can you hear me? Morgan has been teaching me how to speak to people far away without comm. Isn't it cool?"

7

———

Low cots lined the walls and stood in rows across the floor of the vast ballroom in the former BI Ambassador's residence in Kingston. Each was occupied by an injured Resistance fighter. While the Alliance had been assaulting one area of the city, the island's Resistance had organized a coordinated attack on another area, squeezing the EAC between them.

Wright surveyed the scene in the ballroom. Unlike the BA's field hospitals, this place seemed ill-equipped and poorly staffed.

The man who had refused to shake hands with him, later grudgingly introducing himself as Devon, stopped a medic carrying a tray of bloody surgical instruments and told her they had eight Royal Marines in need of treatment.

She did a double-take, looking from Devon to Wright and back, before pursing her lips with disapproval. However, she didn't protest, only nodded before continuing with her task.

Devon's group had led the survivors in Wright's platoon through streets still boiling with skirmishes to this small quarter under Resistance control. The fight for Kingston was a long way from over yet.

Wright said, "I can't tell you how much I appreciate—"

Devon cut him off with a swiftly upraised hand. "This is only until your men are stabilized and you can reunite with your forces on the other side of the city."

"I understand, and I'm grateful."

He actually didn't understand. Not fully. He'd *thought* they were both fighting on the same side. The man's frank animosity was puzzling. But he didn't push it. For whatever reason, the Resistance had rescued his platoon from a hopeless situation. Maybe they just hated the EAC a tad more than they hated the Alliance.

"I'll leave you to organize your troops," said Devon. "You might find some empty rooms in the building where they can rest, but we can't help you with any supplies. We're low as it is."

"It's fine," said Wright. "I get it. Maybe we can find something to do to help you."

The Resistance leader's expression remained impassive in response to the offer, as if he would believe it when he saw it. Without another word, he left.

Wright had left the platoon in the marble-floored lobby of the building among the oil paintings of previous ambassadors, sliced, ripped, and daubed with graffiti. He now ordered that his injured Marines be brought into the ballroom.

His men and women were all traumatized and tired after their long fight. They needed rest, but he wouldn't allow them more than an hour or two. They also needed to stay active. It would keep them from dwelling on the events of the devastating engagement they'd survived. There would be time for grief and nightmares when everything was over.

The medic returned with two others to triage his injured, who had now appeared, carried or walking supported by other Marines. After ordering the healthy remainder to find a spot where they wouldn't be in anyone's way, he replaced his helmet and went outside. It was time to take stock and make his report to Carol.

He perched on a low wall at the bottom of the wide steps that led down to street level. The street was empty of life, and the sun was rising on a city of smoke and ruddy haze. He brought up the list of dead on his HUD. One fatality was too many, and here were Elphicke, Patel, and twelve more good men and women who had given their lives. Men and women? Most of them had barely lived, and— He closed his eyes. He couldn't allow himself to dwell on the deaths.

He comm'd Carol.

"What are you doing, Major?" the officer interrupted in the middle of Wright's update. "I ordered you to join the rest of the troops regrouping at the Prime Minister's Palace."

"We aren't able to reach it, sir. The EAC control the intervening territory."

"I see, well—"

"The Resistance are helping us out. They rescued us, and they've taken us to their field hospital."

"The Resistance? We've been having problems coordinating with them. It's lucky they were in the right place to help you."

"Very lucky. Sir, I think they're not entirely on board with the Alliance retaking Jamaica."

"You don't say? That doesn't make a lot of sense. Are you sure? What's the alternative? Do they want to remain living under the control of the EAC?"

"From what I can tell, they seem to want independence. But I only spoke to one of the leaders briefly."

Carol hotly retorted, "If they think they're going to win back Jamaica without our help, they're living in cloud cuckoo land."

"Maybe, sir, but—"

"We'll be damned if we're going to liberate them just to hand over valuable territory to their control. Sit tight, Major. I may need you to do some digging and find out more about their intentions."

Carol cut the comm.

Wright wondered if he'd said too much. The Jamaicans would never win back their land without the Alliance's help. On the other hand, the BA's military was under the impression it was fighting for one of its own territories. If Devon represented the opinion of the majority of the Resistance, the two forces had opposite aims.

He could see the Jamaicans' viewpoint. If they wanted autonomy, they should have it. But it did seem kind of underhand to allow the Britannic Alliance to expend its people and arms on winning a war when they wouldn't benefit from it.

He heaved a sigh. Let the higher ups sort it out. He would focus on doing his job.

The sun was a little higher, illuminating a scene of devastation. In his passage through the city, he didn't think he'd seen a single intact window near ground level. Looters or armed conflict had taken out everything for the first two or three stories. Scorches left by pulse rounds covered walls, abandoned, burned out vehicles littered the streets, and bomb sites punctuated rows of buildings.

Summoning the energy from an unknown place, Wright rose from the wall and wearily climbed the steps to the Ambassador's Residence. He wanted to find out how his injured were doing. He wasn't sure how long he could rely on the kindness of the Resistance, given its feelings about the BA.

As he was walking between two rows of cots, trying to find his Marines, he spotted Devon. He was walking down the next row, talking to a white man. Both were using the local language.

Wright halted in surprise. He recognized the man Devon was talking to, but he couldn't place him. It was odd that he should know him at all. This was only the second time he'd been in Jamaica, and the first time he'd also been on duty, attempting to assassinate Dwyr Orr. But Devon's companion didn't look like military.

He scoured his brain for several moments before he made the connection. He hadn't seen the man in real life, but in vidnews reports. He was looking at Hans Jonte, head of SIS.

Jonte looked older and thinner than Wright remembered him. Gray thickly speckled his overgrown black hair and beard, and his features were lined and hollowed. His worn, stained clothes were also a far cry from the smart business suits government officials wore, but Wright was positive he was correct. What ordeals had the man endured? It must have been quite a feat to survive the Crusaders' invasion.

Noticing he was being stared at, Jonte quit his conversation with Devon and came over.

"Major Wright?" he asked.

"Yes, I—"

"As soon as your injured are treated, be prepared to move on, Major."

Taken aback, Wright didn't immediately reply. He'd expected Jonte to be relieved to make contact with someone from the BA military, but he appeared irritated.

"You have to understand," Jonte went on, "our resources are extremely stretched. It isn't in our interest to be helping allies whose aims aren't completely aligned with our own."

Our resources? *Our* interest?

"Sorry," Wright replied, "but I'm confused. Aren't you Hans Jonte?"

"That's correct. Your confusion is understandable, but I no longer work for the BA government. I represent the Jamaican Resistance now."

"Right, well, nothing would suit me better than to reunite with the rest of the BA forces. We'll be out of your hair just as soon as we can."

"Thanks."

With that, Jonte left him.

The former head of SIS was now working for the Jamaican Resistance? Wright filed the fact under 'Not My Business' and continued to search for his injured.

HE DISCOVERED one of them recovering from emergency surgery. The doc said the woman wouldn't be safe to move for at least a week. The other seven had less serious injuries and would be locomotive, with help, in a couple of days. With the Resistance holding the south of the city, the BA the north, and the EAC holding the sector in between, the platoon was stuck where it was for the time being anyway.

He ordered his uninjured Marines to make themselves useful to the Resistance in whatever way they could, whether it was helping to move patients or supplies, finding sources of food, or searching for the missing. He spent his time tending to the needs of his recovering men and women to ease the burden on the medical staff.

By the third night in the hospital, Wright had almost forgotten about his strange encounter with Hans Jonte. He hadn't seen the man again, and his mind was focused on dealing with the current situation. Then, that evening when he was outside in the Ambassador's grounds, Jonte approached him.

"I hope you didn't mind me being rather brusque with you the other day," he said. "You have to understand my position here is delicate."

"Not a problem, Mr Jonte. Devon had already made it clear the Resistance was only prepared to go so far to help us. I'll be moving the platoon on as soon as it's safe."

"I'm sure Devon would appreciate it. Um..." He checked their surroundings. No one else was nearby. "When you're finally face to face with your CO, Major, there's something I'd like you to do for me. Could you pass on a message? I'd prefer you didn't say anything over comm. You never know who might pick it up."

Wright's eyebrows rose. "Our encryption is tight, sir."

Jonte gave a half smile. "Probably not as much as you think. The message is to be passed on to the new chiefs of staff. I want them to know I'm still alive and continuing the work of the Alliance in Jamaica."

Wright's eyebrows rose higher. "But you said—"

"I said what was expedient in the situation. Devon could overhear us, you see. I have to be careful. But I *am* still loyal to the BA. I want the people in power to know that. I hope I don't need to spell it out that this is to be kept strictly between us."

"Whatever you say, Mr Jonte. I'll pass on the message."

"Thank you."

8

———————

Lorcan paced outside Iolani Hale's cabin, his hands clasped behind his back, waiting for her to emerge. She'd refused to return to the suite she'd been confined to when she first arrived on the *Bres*, so he'd given her another, one of the best. It had seemed only fair after his earlier treatment of her. Though he could be ruthless in his business dealings, resorting to kidnapping had been a moment of madness. He regretted his actions—most especially since the upshot had been he was forced to take her on as a consultant.

Ever since the day when Kekoa had tried to help her escape and he'd agreed to her proposal, he'd avoided her. The embarrassment and awkwardness were too raw. But the situation could not go on forever. He had to make use of her in the manner she'd dictated, sooner or later.

His attitude toward the world-renowned zoologist had altered radically. Not so long ago, he'd *wanted* her to share her knowledge and advice with him. He'd sought her out to invite her to participate in the Project, to help fulfill humanity's destiny of colonizing the galaxy. Yet now she was here...

The door slid open, revealing Hale dressed in the informal ship's uniform of pale gray tunic and slacks. Staff could wear whatever they wanted, but these clothes from the ship's printers were free to all and most didn't bother wearing anything else.

She tilted her head back to meet his gaze and, as always, he found her frank stare uncomfortable. Clearly, it would be a very long time before she forgave or forgot what he'd done.

"I got your message," she said, "and I replied. Didn't you see it? There's no need for you to accompany me. I know my way around the ship very well."

"So you've settled in?" he asked, deciding to overlook her slight rudeness. He'd thought he was being kind in escorting her to the meeting.

"I guess so. It isn't home and it never will be, but after a few weeks here, I'm finally getting used to the place."

"I imagine it must feel very different from your home in the jungle. Life aboard a starship isn't for everyone. Some find it taxing. If it gets too much for you, don't forget you're free to visit the habitats at any time. The ones that are up and running, that is. Kekoa can tell you which they are."

"Thanks. I've already visited a few as part of my investigation into the Project."

"I hope you found them up to standard."

She gave him a look. She'd clearly found the habitats anything but up to standard. However, all she said, was, "Let's save that conversation for the meeting, okay?"

Lorcan tensed his jaw, uncomfortable that she wouldn't tell him her findings immediately. If there was something important to know, he'd didn't want it sprung on him in front of his staff. "Ms Hale—"

"Iolani is fine. We're going to be working closely together so the less bullshit the better, Lorcan."

"I can't disagree with that. But what I wanted to say is—"

Iolani abruptly halted and her hand flew to her ear. Her features became suffused with joy.

"Yes, that's right. Thanks! I'll be right there."

As if suddenly remembering she wasn't alone, she said to Lorcan, "Sorry, I'm going to be late for the meeting. A delivery I've been waiting for just arrived. I have to go to the shuttle bay."

"Can't it wait?" Lorcan asked, but she was already trotting away from him and she didn't reply, though she must have heard him.

He went after her, wondering what she was so excited about. The meeting couldn't start until she was there anyway. As he walked quickly in her wake, he comm'd the others to let them know about the delay. Had she ordered some scientific equipment? Her passion for her discipline was well known and would explain her sudden happiness.

Only one of the *Bres's* passenger shuttle bays was currently operational, its capacity sufficient to cope with the movements of staff arriving and leaving the ship. When the prospective colonists began to arrive, six more would open to cope with the influx. Cargo shipments of construction materials formed the majority of arrivals, and they went to whichever landing dock was closest to the site where they were to be used.

If Iolani had ordered equipment, it had to be small and probably fragile to be shipped via a shuttle intended for personnel. Lorcan's interest was piqued. He'd long had a fascination for the intricate, complex machinery scientists used in their experiments.

The light above the bay doors turned green, and Iolani rushed between them the second they began to draw apart.

The snub-nosed, narrow-winged, forty-seater shuttle stood on its pad, clamps securing it. The hatch opened, and the first of the passengers began descending the steps.

Iolani broke from a trot to a run as she crossed the steel floor of the bay.

Lorcan halted, puzzled. What could possibly be so important to the woman? Then it hit him. It wasn't equipment that had arrived, it was a person. Her boyfriend, or maybe a family member had come to stay with her.

He was a little put out he hadn't been consulted about the unauthorized guest, but he couldn't begrudge her the company. As he knew too well, life aboard the *Bres* could be awfully lonely. It would make her stay more tolerable. He resumed walking. It wouldn't hurt to meet the newcomer and introduce himself.

At the front of the shuttle, a smaller hatch for the pilot and crew opened.

A bark rang out and echoed around the cavernous bay.

He stopped again.

Not a person...

Iolani's two massive dogs leapt from the crew hatch. They jumped directly to the bay floor, bypassing the steps entirely. Iolani was twenty meters from them, and they covered the distance in about four bounds.

She wisely sank to her knees—the animals could easily topple the small woman in their enthusiasm—and she was soon surrounded by a blur of ecstatic dogs' bodies. She rubbed their flanks and heads and nuzzled them, her face wet, either from their licks or her tears or perhaps both.

Lorcan watched, his hands on his hips. His experience of the woman's pets had been terrifying, and he was not happy they were aboard his ship. If she'd asked him for permission to have them there, he would have probably said no, which, of course, was why she hadn't asked him.

How had she discovered where they were being kept? The question provoked greater annoyance. Only a couple of trusted staff members knew which animal rescue center in Suriname he'd tasked with collecting and caring for the animals. That meant that, not only had Iolani gone behind his back to order the shipping of her dogs, one of his employees had colluded with her. If there was one thing he despised among the people whose wages he paid, it was disloyalty.

He had an uncomfortable feeling of control slipping from his grasp. Iolani had questioned his morals and the scientific basis of the Project. Now she was undermining his authority too.

He sourly watched the joyful reunion, waiting for it to be over. Some moments later, she finally noticed him.

"Uh, sorry." She rose to her feet, calming her dogs with shushes and pats. "I didn't know you were here," she went on. "I'll take Darwin and Banks to my cabin. I won't be long."

She stepped past him with the animals flanking her, their claws tapping on the metal.

His glare followed.

When he arrived at the meeting room, animated chatter was leaking through the doorway. He couldn't quite make out what was being said, but he could take a good guess. At his appearance, everyone became silent and became deeply interested in the table surface as he entered and sat down.

"Ms Hale will join us in a few minutes."

Kekoa, Steadman, and Jurrah were present, as well as Xiao, the Cryosuspension Director, and Bourke, who Lorcan had recently promoted to Head of Security. He'd sacked the previous head after he let Hale escape.

Had Bourke been the one who'd told Iolani of the location of her dogs?

He fixed his gaze on the man, but Bourke had become fascinated with the grid covering the air circulation duct.

"Can I say..." Steadman piped up "...I didn't receive an agenda. Just checking there isn't one."

"That's right," Lorcan replied. "This meeting is to formally welcome Ms Hale to the team and to explore how she'll fit in as we go forward."

Kekoa idly scrolled the interface embedded in the tabletop. She was the main person responsible for the situation with Hale. She'd helped release the woman from her suite. If it hadn't been for Kekoa, Iolani would be safely in cryo by now, not sticking her nose into his business and interfering with his plans.

He drummed his fingertips.

Waiting for Hale was extremely irritating.

The door opened, and everyone looked up.

"Sorry I'm late." Iolani quickly slid into a seat.

"So glad you could finally make it," said Lorcan acidly. "Welcome to the Antarctic Project, Ms Hale. I'm sure we will have many happy and fulfilling days working with you."

Kekoa softly coughed.

"Let's not waste time on introductions," he continued. "Ms Hale's reputation precedes her, and I'm sure she has been aboard long enough for everyone to have made her acquaintance. As you probably know she'll be acting as scientific adviser on various aspects of the Project, wherever her expertise is most beneficial. Let's begin. From earlier conversations, I believe your first endeavor will be to work with Kekoa on assessing the habitats?" He addressed his final comment to Iolani.

"No," she replied flatly. Addressing the room, she continued, "I've spent the last few weeks looking at everything you're doing here. I can see the vast amount of planning and work that's gone on. So when I say what must be said, I don't want anyone here to take it as a slight on their professional abilities. I've been forced to come to the conclusion that the Project is deeply flawed. It isn't your work that's the problem, it's the concept. The premise of what you're attempting is wrong."

She paused.

Her comments were being met with blank stares.

Lorcan was shocked too, but he was also trying hard to control his rage. How *dare* she criticize the Project? She was striking at the heart of everything he believed in, his life's work. And she knew it. The little viper. She was clearly out to get revenge for what he'd done to her.

"Have you *quite* finished?" he said between his teeth.

"Lorcan, I've barely started." She folded her hands in her lap. "In fact, it's hard to know where *to* begin. The idea that millions of people are paying huge sums of money to be taken on this fool's errand..." She paused once more. "I won't go on. It isn't helpful to be negative, and, anyway, the Project is too far advanced to cancel. The best I can offer is remedial action. We'll have to hope to God enough people survive for the colonization to not be a complete disaster."

He had no words.

"You have identified, I think, three potential planets?" She looked to Lorcan for confirmation, but he could only return her gaze, slack-mouthed. "Let me guess—their gravities are close to Earth's and the composition of their atmospheres is very similar too. Maybe you also have an idea about the land mass/ocean ratios. I don't know. The point I want to emphasize is, none of that really matters. What everyone seems to be forgetting is that these planets are *alien*. They are not new Edens waiting for the blessing of humankind to descend and grace them with their presence."

"That's enough!" Lorcan managed to finally spit out. "Your implication of naivety is insulting. I don't know where you got your impression, but it isn't accurate."

"I apologize," Hale replied. "I don't mean to cause offense, but I'm trying to shock you into understanding just how unprepared you are. Let me give you an example. Have you considered how the human body will react to an entirely alien environment? It could easily be provoked into a profound and devastating immune reaction. Even attempting to breathe the planet's air, with its unfamiliar microbes, spores, and dust, could result in anaphylactic shock and death."

She let this sink in, watching the stunned faces.

"Assuming by some miracle your colonists' immune systems don't go into overdrive immediately, you're going to have to hope they can eat the planet's organisms without a reaction. Why? Because the chance you can get Earth flora and fauna to grow there is practically zero. As I explained to Lorcan not so long ago when he came to see me in Suriname, the systems that support life here on Earth are incredibly complex. We scientists have only just begun to appreciate that fact, let alone understand the systems themselves. I would lay everything I own on the probability that anything you try to plant in an alien soil will die, and any animal species you set free in the new environment will do the same. They won't stand a chance. Of course, you can grow things like tomatoes and lettuce with hydroponics, but staples like cereals? Forget it. You need friendly soil."

Lorcan swallowed.

Silence reigned.

"What can we do?" Kekoa choked out. "You said the Project has gone too far to stop now. If we're going to kill millions of people, I don't want to be a part of it."

"I understand," Iolani replied. "Neither do I. Yet here we both are." She turned to Lorcan. "These are the two most significant flaws I've identified. There are many, many others, but they'll have to wait. We need to focus on these two first. On the plus side, I don't think they're insurmountable. If I did, I would have left already. There's a chance I can do something to help if I get some more experts on board. I have some contacts in human immunology I'd like to approach. There are treatments that suppress the immune system. They increase the likelihood of cancer and if we use them it would mean you absolutely cannot take any communicable diseases along with you.

"As to the problem with establishing Earth species so the colonists have something safe to eat...the ethics and dangers of doing that on an alien planet aside...I have an idea how to solve it. The solution involves genetic engineering, something I can do myself, but I will need colleagues to work with. I have a few people in mind.

"I don't want to go through some massive rigmarole to get the people I need here. I have to have the freedom to operate independently on both these problems, without any interference. Do you agree?"

Lorcan held her gaze, wanting, *needing*, something to say in retaliation to her challenge to his authority. But nothing came to him.

"Keep me updated on your progress, Ms Hale."

He rose stiffly and stalked out of the meeting. Once he was safely alone in the passageway, he halted. The walls seemed to be flowing toward and away from him. He thought he might faint. He took deep breaths and waited for the dizziness to fade. When he thought he could walk without the danger of falling, he went straight to his suite and didn't emerge again that day.

9

———

Wrapped in her sleeping bag and ground sheet, Taylan lay at the foot of an ancient oak. She alternated between shivering with cold and clutching her coverings around her, and then throwing them off when she grew unbearably hot. Her right thigh was a bundle of fire, her leg useless. She taken the last of the antibiotics in her first aid kit days previously. The short course might have fixed an infected cut or even incipient pneumonia, but a large injury from a pulse round was beyond its scope. Her food had also run out days ago, but she had no appetite anyway.

In a moment of clarity, she reached out to lift and shake her water bottle. It felt about a quarter full. Feeling about with her fingertips, her hand alighted on the pack of sterilizer tablets. All the blisters were empty.

Another wave of shivering hit her, and she shut her eyes. Her mind wandered.

She was back on the hill near the orphanage, cutting the throats of the Crusaders who had tried to capture her. Their blood still crusted her clothes. So much blood. So much death.

She was with Patrin and Kayla in the pocket handkerchief

of a garden outside their tiny, terraced house. She was throwing a ball for Patrin to catch while Kayla made a daisy chain. The sun was hot on her back.

She was in the West BI Resistance hideout, preparing to leave. The members moved around her, shadowy in the half-darkness under the hill. They brought her items for her expedition, which she stowed in her backpack. The mood was somber. One of the group came to speak to her.

She cut him off before he could speak. "I know what you're going to say."

The serious, guarded look on his face had said it all already.

"It doesn't matter," she continued. "I have to do this."

"Taylan, I'm begging you, think again," he urged.

His name was Meilyr, and he was the eldest of four brothers. All athletically built, pale-skinned, dark-haired and dark-eyed, their kinship was evident to anyone who saw them together. Angharad's sons, they were among the founders of the Resistance in that part of the BI.

"We've only survived this long because we stick together," he said. "If you go out there alone, who'll keep watch while you sleep? If you get in trouble, who'll help you fight off your attackers?"

"I can look after myself," she replied. "Probably better than you think."

"I'm sure that's true. It doesn't change the fact that it's dangerous to be out there on your own. If the Crusaders catch you..." He didn't complete his sentence.

Taylan didn't need him to elaborate. She'd seen what Dwyr Orr had done to Wilson, and she didn't doubt Meilyr had his own tales to tell about what had happened to Resistance members who fell into the madwoman's hands. He was just looking out for her.

She touched his shoulder. "Meilyr, until I find my kids I'll never be able to rest. I gave up the search once and it was torture. If I stop looking, how can I live with myself?"

"Many of us have lost—"

"If Angharad had been separated from you, do you think she would have given up trying to find you again?"

He nodded reluctantly. "She wouldn't. I can't deny it."

It was all that needed to be said. She continued to push items into her backpack.

"Lots of children went missing in the early days of the invasion," said Meilyr. "A few were found. I hope you return soon with your kids."

She gave him a tight-lipped smile. She certainly hoped to see him again too, but not without Kayla and Patrin by her side.

In the hour before dawn the next day, while the others were all asleep, she'd slipped away. Though she'd only known the Resistance fighters a short time they felt like kin. Goodbyes would be too painful.

Dragged back to the present by a wave of agony from her leg, Taylan reflected she would give a lot to see Meilyr again.

She would also give a lot to see Wright. What was the earnest major doing? Before she'd left the hideout, she'd heard the BA had launched a full-scale offensive in Jamaica. He was probably somewhere there, leading his Marines into battle. What an idiot she'd been to try to kiss him. Yet she didn't regret it. Underneath his rigid formality, he was a sweet guy. It was a shame she'd probably never see him again.

A fresh surge of pain welled up in her thigh. She grimaced, squeezing her eyelids together tightly.

As the wave passed, a voice sounded in her head.

"Corporal Ellis, this is Brigadier Colbourn."

What the f—

Her implant! She was still carrying around the goddamned Royal Marines' implant in her head.

"What do you want?" she hissed.

Surely it was dangerous for the brigadier to comm her? The Crusaders might pick up the signal and figure out her location.

"The discharge you were given is invalid, Ellis. You're still serving as a Royal Marine. I want you to—"

"No," Taylan gasped. "I'm not a bloody Marine and I don't give a shit what you want me to do." She let fly a further string of expletives, finishing with, "Stop comming me, or you're going to get me killed."

Silence.

She lay rigid, outrage consuming her. Colbourn had always been a bitch, but this was beyond the pale.

Her fury bringing her to full consciousness, she took stock of her surroundings. Some hours seemed to have passed since she'd last been fully awake. Her most recent memory was of streaks of sunset colors filling the sky through the tree canopy. The colors had been replaced by twinkling pinpoints of light in a black void.

How much longer did she have before the infection entered her blood and sepsis killed her? She guessed not much more than a day or so, if the process hadn't already begun.

Two alternatives stood before her: Stay where she was and let death take her, or try to move. The latter choice was the less rosy. It would probably also end with dying, just more painfully. But, despite everything, she wasn't ready to let go of the thread of hope that she could find Kayla and Patrin.

She unwrapped the ground sheet from around her shoulders and then pushed down her sleeping bag. The influx of cool night air on her body instantly set her off shivering again. Doing her best to ignore her discomfort, she slowly pulled herself into a sitting position, and then packed only her most essential items.

Panting and weeping with pain, she leaned to her right and grabbed the crutch she'd roughly crafted from a hazel branch. Using it as a prop along with the oak tree's trunk, she managed to get onto her good foot. She inserted the crutch under her armpit.

Her left leg hung free as she brought the crutch forward. Leaning heavily on it, she hopped a step on her left leg. Another shift of the crutch, and another hop. So far, so good.

Something about what she was doing—the night air on her face and infiltrating her clothes, the exercise, or the short sleep —brought a sharpness to her mind she hadn't experienced for days. The surrounding woodland appeared clear and defined in the moonlight, and her ears were picking up minor nocturnal noises of animals moving through the undergrowth.

Perhaps it was only that she was near death. She'd heard the dying often rallied in their final hours, feeling better than they had for days.

Move the crutch, hop. Move the crutch, hop.

10

"Move out," ordered Wright.

After five days' wait, his platoon was finally leaving the Resistance field hospital. An ambulance would be arriving at some point for the Marine who'd undergone surgery, but everyone else faced a three-kilometer walk across Kingston to the rendezvous point. From there, they would travel by shuttle to the *Gallant*.

The battle for Jamaica was over, to all intents and purposes. The Alliance had won. Yet no one seemed overjoyed by the victory. As the Marines walked from the former Ambassador's Residence, their backs were bent and their rifles held loosely.

Wright's morale was low too. So many had died, and not only in his own platoon. He'd heard the Alliance's losses had been heavy. And for what? During their time at the hospital, the Jamaicans had been cold and distant, barely tolerating the platoon's presence. It wasn't like he'd expected overwhelming gratitude, but—as far as he knew—none of the men or women under his command were from around here. They'd risked their lives and died in order to free a country not their own. He didn't think a little friendliness would have been too much to ask.

He was not interested in politics or current affairs. He'd decided long ago that the Alliance was a force for good and fighting in its military was morally right. After that, he'd been content to follow orders. So he didn't know what the Jamaicans' beef with the Alliance was. Maybe it was justified. Still, it seemed unfair that the locals would take out their animosity on individuals who were trying to help them.

On the other hand, Devon's group had saved the platoon from certain annihilation.

The leader had also shown Wright a route across the city that would take them through the safest areas. The mopping-up process was ongoing, and pockets of Crusaders were holding out, refusing to surrender. His Marines were battle-weary and he didn't want to put them into any more conflict situations if he could avoid it. Carol hadn't given him anywhere near such detailed intel. Despite their animosity, Wright trusted Devon's information more anyway. The Resistance's knowledge of the city and what was happening within it was intimate.

"Major Wright!"

It was Hans Jonte. He hadn't seen the former head of SIS since they'd met in the garden.

Jonte descended the steps at the front of the residence. Wright waited, allowing the platoon to go on without him.

When Jonte reached him, he looked over his shoulder at the Residence before continuing, "I just wanted to check—"

"I know," said Wright. "The message. I haven't forgotten."

"Good. Thank you. I can't tell you how fortunate it's been for me that you happened to come here. It's very difficult to..." He struggled for the appropriate word.

"Play two sides?" Wright offered.

The former Alliance official looked somewhat embarrassed.

"I suppose you could put it like that. But it's for the greater good."

Wright was tired. Bone tired. Too tired for the man's intrigues. "Well, I'd better go. I hope whatever greater good it is you're aiming for, you get it." He began to move away.

"For the greater good of all, of course."

Wright didn't answer.

"Safe journey, Major!" Jonte called out.

Wright wasn't stupid enough to imagine the man actually cared about his well-being. He only cared that he didn't die before passing on the message. But Jonte's words reminded him of someone else who had wished him a safe journey not so long ago, in a hollow in a hill in West BI.

He picked up his pace to catch up to his platoon and continued walking fast until he reached the front. They had a long boulevard to traverse, which would lead them into the city center. From there, they had to head east. The route wasn't the most direct, but Devon had warned them to steer clear of an area that housed a sports stadium. It was here the majority of Crusaders were concentrated, entirely surrounded by Alliance troops. Negotiations had been attempted but met with silence.

Should blow the whole lot of them up, Devon had said, disgusted.

Wright could sympathize. He expected tales of execution sites and mass graves to come out soon. That was what had happened in every other place the EAC had invaded. He didn't see why Jamaica should be any different.

Carol comm'd him. After the usual preliminaries, he said, "I want you to make a short diversion. There are seventeen soldiers in a bad way about half a klick from you. They're only just out of Basic, have no officers with them, and several are injured. I want you to collect them and take them to the rendezvous. I'm sending coordinates."

The numbers appeared on Wright's HUD.

He mentally sighed. He didn't object to lending the Army a hand, but the men and women in need of help were near the sports stadium Devon had advised him to avoid. "Roger wilco," he replied.

"See you for debriefing on the *Gallant* in a couple of days," said Carol before closing the comm.

Wright ordered his platoon to halt. He picked Bates, Snowdon, and three more uninjured Marines to take with him, and then told the rest to find somewhere safe to wait until he returned.

The route to the soldiers took them through downtown Kingston. Like everywhere else he'd seen in the war-torn city, the place was devastated. Looters had ripped the place apart, and battles with the EAC had finished the job.

The stadium rose above the skyline. Miraculously still intact, it was testament to modernity, its lines sleek and silver, glinting in the brilliant sunshine. The contrast with the ransacked, demolished corrugated iron and wooden shacks of the poor sector they were walking through was stunning. Helis were circling the skies over the stadium, and Wright had no doubt the Alliance would be flooding the place with survi-drones as they assessed the situation. He wondered how many Crusaders were holed up in there.

They found the soldiers in the shadow of two huge shade trees in a square. Most had their backs propped against the trunks, some lay at full stretch on the dirt. There were a few half-hearted responses to the Marines' approach, but the men and women were clearly spent. What a baptism into military life they must have had, straight from Basic into full-blown warfare. He guessed they were all barely adults too. The Alliance was becoming more and more desperate in its search for new recruits.

Wright told the ones who had stood and saluted they were at ease, and then began assessing the group. Distant sounds of voice amplifiers could be heard as the Alliance negotiators tried to talk the Crusaders into surrendering.

He looked at the ones lying down, while Bates and the other Marines chatted to the rest. Veterans of several battles, they knew the gentle banter that would help the teenagers heal psychologically from their experiences.

He ran a medical scan on the first recumbent soldier. Private Kelly Mapple: Fractured humerus, multiple hematomas, third-degree burns to the stomach, low blood pressure but no internal bleeding, ninety-one percent chance of full recovery with medical treatment within the next eight hours. "Are you able to walk, soldier?" he asked.

"Yes, sir," she replied. "I think so."

"Good." He ordered Snowdon to assist Private Mapple.

He felt sick. The young woman reminded him of Patel. The Alliance docs would patch her up and send her back into battle, a lamb to the slaughter.

Pushing through his misgivings, he moved to the next injured soldier.

The sky lit up.

Brighter even than the tropical sunlight, a flash burst from the direction of the stadium. At the same moment, an explosion roared through the air. Wright didn't have time to order the soldiers and Marines to take cover before the shockwave hit. Ripping the trees out of the ground, the wave blew him across the street and into a wall.

His helmet saved his head from the worst of the impact, and luckily he hadn't lifted his visor to talk to Mapple. The people in his care had been similarly tossed like rag dolls by the detonation.

He lifted his gaze to the skyline. The stadium had disappeared and in its place was a rising cloud of smoke and dust.

What had happened?

The Alliance would not have ordered an air strike on the

place, not while negotiations were being attempted and it had so many personnel in the immediate area. The AP? The act seemed senseless. Ua Talman had little to gain by bombing the site and antagonizing two forces that opposed him. And the Resistance was unlikely to possess a weapon capable of inflicting that level of damage. That only left the EAC. The trapped Crusaders had either blown themselves up rather than surrender, or the Dwyr had ordered the annihilation of her own troops. Both were possible.

Wright looked around him, scanning the Marines and soldiers. Several were unmoving.

He opened his visor, turned onto his hands and knees, and vomited into the dust.

11

Kala leaned forward, propped her elbows on a table, and rested her forehead on her fingertips. She was sitting in the *Belladonna's* mess, facing Perran.

Everything seemed to be falling apart. Jamaica and Barbados were lost to her—two major Caribbean islands and thousands of military personnel. Reports from the other islands she held were either bad or missing. She suspected she'd lost more of her territory, only the relevant military leaders were dead or the situation was too chaotic to get information out.

One thing she did know for sure: faced with being taken prisoner by the Alliance, the troops trapped in Kingston had destroyed themselves. Their final message had reached her half an hour ago. It had been the right thing for them to do. Nevertheless, she felt their loss. Despite her exhortation to her people to reproduce, the numbers she could devote to warfare were decreasing every year.

She was beset on all fronts, and she didn't know what to do. Should she divert the forces she'd massed in the BI to the Caribbean? It would take days for the majority of them to get there, and by then it would probably be too late. Should she press ahead with the invasion of Ireland despite the damage the BI Resistance had done to her military infrastructure?

Or would her time be better spent focusing on the challenges she faced here aboard her flagship?

It was between regular meal times, and the mess was nearly empty. She'd brought Perran here supposedly for cocoa—the chef could whip up a more delicious drink than that created by the food replicators—but in fact she hoped to avoid Morgan. The last place she would look for them would be somewhere frequented by the ship's crew, knowing Kala's distaste for over-familiarity with her inferiors.

"I want to go home," Perran whined.

Kala tutted. Though she loved him dearly, sometimes her son could be vexing. But she suppressed her irritation. As well as her military problems on the surface, she was fighting a personal war. It was a subtle battle for Perran's affection. This one, she was determined to win.

"Which home do you mean?" she asked, reaching out to brush away a stray hair that hung over his eyes. "We have so many."

"The last one. By the harbor. I made a friend there and I miss her." His lower lip jutted.

"I'm sure your friend will wait for you to come back," Kala replied.

"That isn't the *point*! I want to play with her. I don't have anyone to play with here. There are only grown-ups, and they aren't any fun."

"But there's so much else to do. Aren't you excited to be aboard a starship?"

"No." He folded his arms across his chest.

"What if I ask one of the weapons officers to show you the particle ray?"

"I don't want to see it."

"Or the chief engineer could show you the engines."

"Why would I be interested in engines?"

"That's fair. I'm not interested in the engines either." She smiled.

He frowned.

Maybe it was time for *the talk*.

"Perran, you're growing up so fast. It won't be long before you're a young man. Have you thought about what that means?"

"I can have a girlfriend?"

"Yes, you can have a girlfriend if that's what you want. You can have your pick. Any girl would consider herself lucky to be with you. But that isn't what I mean. You know I'm the Crusade Leader. As my son, you'll have a role to play when you're a little older. An important role, second only to my own. And when I die, you'll take over from me."

She paused, watching for his reaction. He didn't seem to be particularly impressed.

"Isn't that exciting?" she asked.

"What will I be able to do?"

"Anything you want, within reason. It's a perk of being the leader."

"So if I wanted to go home right now, I could?"

"Yes, but you would have to consider whether that was wise. It isn't in our best interests to return to Earth now. So although we could, we aren't."

"Why isn't it in our best interests?"

At last, he was beginning to think things through. "Because some people want to hurt us. It's safer if we remain on the ship for a while until the danger's over."

"You mean that man with the sword? Is he the one who wants to hurt us?"

Kala grimaced. Perran had witnessed Arthur's murderous

approach through the crowd on the quayside at the invasion launch ceremony. "Yes, him, and a few others."

"We should kill them."

"We should and we will, in time. Until then, we need to stay here. Do you understand?"

With some apparent reluctance, Perran gave a short nod. He picked up his mug of cocoa and sipped.

Kala was pleased. She hadn't expected the conversation to take the turn it had, but it had been for the best in the end. Perhaps she'd shielded her son too much from the reality of life leading the EAC. He was more mature than she'd thought.

Compared to her other problems it was a small win, but she was grateful for it nonetheless.

12

Jamaica had been won. Now, for Hans, the hard work began.

As he prepared to leave the cave in the mountains for the last time, he hoped the Royal Marines' major he'd met could be relied upon to pass on his message. Support from the BA's military wing would be instrumental to his return to a position of influence. Ties between SIS and the Alliance's armed forces had been strong in the past. When SIS eventually rose from the ashes they would be so again.

But he couldn't risk approaching the new military heads directly. They were not the type of people one could approach unnoticed, and he was confident the Resistance were observing him closely. Mariya had warned him many Jamaicans would never overcome their distrust of the backra.

He lifted the heavy, old-fashioned pulse rifle that had been his constant companion since the attack on the EAC headquarters. Would he ever need the weapon again? He hoped not, but the situation on the island remained chaotic. Crusader troops were still being hunted down and rounded up, though he guessed as the news of the Resistance/BA victory spread, many would take their own lives.

He surveyed the rest of his meager belongings in the cave: clothes, a blanket, water bottle, camping utensils and other items, all scrounged after being released from his cage, all dirty, old, and worn. He didn't need these things. Why had he bothered to come here? Better everyday articles could be found among the wreckage of Kingston. So many of the city's inhabitants had been murdered, though food was now scarce, it was awash with other goods, too many even for the looters to handle.

"Are you ready, Hans?" Devon asked from the cave entrance where he stood waiting.

"I'll be there in a minute."

The wide space was nearly empty of people. Members of the group he'd lived with for weeks had mostly already departed, taking their most treasured possessions with them.

He suddenly realized why he'd wanted to come back one last time.

He walked to a small alcove under a jutting overhang. The items here were undisturbed. A blanket was folded neatly on top of a pillow. A few items of cloth were stacked in an orderly pile. He squatted down and opened a small backpack. Inside were personal things: a comb, a silver necklace, several photographs. He pulled one out and held it up to look at it more closely in the beam from his flashlight.

It was an image of two sisters, their arms wrapped around each other's shoulders. They were standing in front of a rundown little house in the countryside, smiling at the camera, their smiles lazy but full of joy. Full of love for each other.

He looked more closely at the identical young women, but he couldn't tell them apart.

He inhaled deeply and then exhaled in a sigh.

Tucking the photo into his breast pocket, he looked into the pack again. He found small ceramic pots filled with lotions and oils. As he opened one, he recognized a medicinal, herbal odor. It was the ointment that had healed the sores he'd developed in his time in the bamboo cage. He put the pot down and picked up another. Sniffing the light oil it held, he was surprised as sudden tears flooded his eyes. His mind only caught up with the visceral, unconscious response a second later.

It was the oil Mariya had used in her hair. He would recognize the scent anywhere.

Rationally, it made no sense he should grieve her so deeply. She'd brought him to the Resistance hideout knowing the terrible torture her people would inflict on him. His experience had left physical and psychological scars that would never disappear. Yet she'd also saved his life. If she hadn't driven him away from his villa on the mountainside, the EAC would have caught him eventually. He could never have survived alone.

He screwed the lid on the pot and slipped it into his other breast pocket. He also took the silver necklace.

Devon had left, and so had everyone else. The cave was empty and silent. Scattered remains from the months the group had spent there were strewn carelessly over the floor. How long would the things stay here, unwanted, undisturbed, forgotten?

Heaving another sigh, he plodded out.

Just beyond the entrance, he paused for a few moments to allow his eyes to adjust to the strong sunlight. Stragglers were leaving the clearing, walking along the path that led upward into the jungle. Devon waited for him on higher ground, next to Mariya's car.

The fire that had burned for many nights on the flat, stone ground was smoldering. Some people had chosen to burn their belongings rather than abandon them.

Devon had spied him and was looking impatient, standing with his hands on his hips.

But Hans had one more thing to do. He searched under the cave overhang.

There it is.

In the shadows stood an open, empty bamboo cage, the canes lashed together with vines. Revulsion and dread had passed through Hans as he spotted it. He strode decisively over and snatched it up. Holding it over his head in both hands, he marched to the fire and threw it on top. The vines charred and smoky tendrils drifted up.

"Hurry up, Hans!" Devon shouted. "It's time to go."

Still, he waited.

The flames were too weak to take hold quickly on the tough bamboo.

Hans swung his pulse rifle forward, took aim, and fired.

It was an hour's drive to Kingston. Charles, the Kingston Resistance leader was meeting them there along with the leaders of other Jamaican Resistance groups. Alliance techs were working on re-establishing the net and it was hoped that, by the time the meeting started, the leaders might be able to speak in real time with their counterparts on Barbados, Cayman, Martinique, and St. Lucia. The EAC had been defeated in all these islands, though on other former BA islands, the fighting was ongoing.

As Devon drove along the dirt road through the forest, Hans considered his next steps. The phase he was entering would be particularly tricky. His goal of uniting the countries that had once belonged to the Britannic Alliance and transforming them into a globe-spanning republic remained a long way off. He had to retain the—somewhat shaky—trust and confidence the Caribbean Resistance currently had in him while at the same time resume his former importance within the BA Government. The two objectives were perfectly opposed, making his task almost impossible.

Waves of excitement and pleasure passed through him. He loved a challenge, and this was the challenge of his life.

Sunlight glinted on a moving object on the road ahead.

"What's that?!" Devon exclaimed. He braked, bringing them to a crunching stop.

Hans recognized the device. He'd seen them before on news reports covering disasters and wars. It stood about thirty centimeters tall and was running toward them on eight or ten articulated legs supporting a small, lozenge-shaped body of smooth metal.

"It's a cadaver sniffer," he explained. "The Alliance must have deployed them."

The automated machine raced down the track. When it reached the car, it climbed over the hood. Its feet tapped on the metal. Without a change in pace it mounted the windscreen, ran over the roof and down onto the trunk. After reaching the road again, it swerved right and disappeared into the vegetation.

"It's looking for bodies?" asked Devon.

"That's right," Hans replied. "When it finds one, it'll transmit the location to a database and then continue searching. Recovery teams will check out the sites later and collect remains for identification and burial or cremation."

"That's..." Devon's nose wrinkled "...helpful, I guess."

"It's just one of the things the Alliance will do to aid Jamaica's recovery."

"Yeah, well, just as long as they don't get the wrong idea. Things won't be going back to how they were."

"Has anyone actually told the BA yet?" Hans asked. "Do they have any reason to imagine things will be different now?"

"Not exactly," Devon replied. "Not yet. It's early days. But they must have an idea. We haven't been friendly with them.

We need to get what we can out of them, in payment for all they've done to Jamaica and the rest of the Caribbean over the years. Then we'll give them the bad news."

Hans wondered how that would go down, but he didn't wonder for long. The BA would never accept the loss of such a vital territory, especially not one they fought so hard to win back. It would mean war.

He glanced at Devon. The Resistance fighters were brave, determined, and patriotic, but they were ordinary men and women, not trained troops. They also lacked the BA's firepower. If they stood up against the Alliance even in its weakened state, the conflict would be short and bloody.

It would be a great pity to see two groups with essentially positive values slug it out with each other.

"What sort of timescale are we talking about?" asked Hans. "For delivering the bad news to the Alliance, I mean."

"Two or three months. We'll have to see how things go."

The timing was insanely ambitious and deluded. The local infrastructure was in tatters, and the Jamaicans didn't have the budget or professional capacity to repair all the damage within years, let alone months. It was also nowhere near enough time for him to get them to accept Alliance control. It had taken him more than a decade to whip up the discontent and dissent among the BA hierarchy sufficiently to trigger the coup.

"It's best to take these things carefully," he said. "Small steps. The Caribbean shouldn't try to run before it can walk."

"I understand what you're saying," Devon replied, "but people are impatient to be free. We've had centuries of living under foreign rule. Now we finally have our chance, and we're going to take it. No more bowing to the backra." His head jerked slightly as he appeared to realize what he'd said.

"Sorry."

"It's okay," Hans said warmly. "I'm glad you don't see me the same way as before." It *did* please him, deeply. If Devon momentarily forgot he was a hated member of the former ruling class, so might other Resistance leaders. That would make his job all the easier. "Still," he went on, "I would caution patience."

"I hear you, Hans. Others might not."

A sign flashed up on the dashboard.

"Ah, great," said Devon. "The net's back." He gave the car their destination, took his hands off the wheel, and rested the back of his head on his laced fingers. The car smoothly took over its own steering.

"Good old Alliance. I'm gonna miss them."

He laughed.

"But not enough to ask them to stay."

13

Taylan had died and gone to Heaven. She knew this because Dad came to see her, and he was long dead. When she was twenty-five and pregnant with Patrin, he and Mam had gone out fishing and a sudden squall had overturned the little boat. Though they were wearing life jackets, by the time the Coast Guard found them Mam had died of exposure. A year to the day later, Dad followed her. The death certificate listed a hemorrhagic stroke as the cause, but Taylan knew better.

When he'd come home after the boating accident, the light had gone out of his eyes. He withdrew into himself. Not even the birth of his grandson raised a genuine smile. It was then Taylan knew it was over for him. His body lived on but his heart and soul had departed with Mam in the freezing, swollen sea that had taken her.

Here in Heaven he was happy again. He would lean over her, his face full of love and concern, asking her how she felt.

She felt...dreamy. Being dead wasn't at all like she'd imagined. And Heaven was way darker than she'd anticipated. If that was where she'd gone, where was the sunlight and where were the angels?

Whenever she'd thought about dying, which wasn't often, she'd guessed it was kind of the same as you'd been before you were born. You just didn't exist anymore. But in fact it was more like being in a constant state of having just woken up. Heaven seemed to be a deep pit lit by flickering lights where people who had gone before you paid occasional visits.

She wondered where Mam was. She would have liked to see her too. But when she tried to ask she couldn't speak. Maybe the ability would come back later. She also couldn't move, though she didn't really mind, not yet anyway. She was content to lie there and see Dad every now and again.

Then, one day, Patrin turned up.

No!

Taylan didn't want to look at him, but when she did she saw he was holding his sister's hand.

Kayla! Patrin! My little ones. What happened to you? Is this why I couldn't find you—because you'd gone ahead of me?

She began to cry and tried to sit up. It was wrong. It wasn't fair that her children had died so young. They'd barely had a chance to live. They would never grow up, never fall in love, never become who they were meant to be. All because Dwyr Orr and the EAC had snatched everything away from them.

Patrin was gone.

He'd been replaced by Dad, who was leaning over her again, holding her shoulders. "Calm down," he was saying. "You'll hurt yourself. Stay still."

He didn't seem to understand how wrong it was that his grand kids had lost their lives so young. She tried to push him away but she was too weak. She opened her mouth to tell him to let go of her that she wanted to see her children, but no sound came out.

"Gotta dose her up again," said Dad to someone out of view. "Go to sleep, Taylan. You'll feel better soon."

THE NEXT TIME she opened her eyes, things looked clearer. A low ceiling hung above her, bare dirt between spaced wooden planks. Plump, white roots snaked across the soil, and in places their desiccated, feathery tips protruded.

It was a strange ceiling to find herself under. Taylan stared at it a while. She felt deeply placid and serene, as if nothing whatsoever could trouble her. Without much disturbance to her peace of mind, she remembered believing she was dead. Now, it appeared that wasn't the case. Unless somehow she'd transferred to a different kind of heaven...

Straining with effort, she managed to lift her head a couple of centimeters.

Semi-darkness met her gaze. The planked ceiling was concave, curving down to meet the floor of the circular chamber. Figures slept at the edges, covered in blankets or inside sleeping bags. A single, dim light hung down in the center, and short-legged camping chairs surrounded a plastic sheet, taking up about a quarter of the room. A few men and women were sitting in the chairs. Another was moving items on a low table.

She was back in the Resistance hideout under the hill, though she had no recollection of getting here.

"She's awake," someone said. "Good morning. You decided to return to the land of the living then?"

The person standing by the table had spoken, but he had his back to the light and Taylan could only make out his silhouette. He strode to her side. Dark, shaggy hair hung over his face, but she still recognized him: Meilyr, Angharad's son.

"I..." she coughed "I thought I'd died."

"You very nearly did. Can I take a look at your leg?"

He moved the cover up her body, and then lifted her foot and knee. His brows knit as he studied the back of her thigh. He gently prodded her wound, making her stiffen and gasp.

"Sorry, we had to wean you off the good stuff. Medical supplies are hard to come by. Your wound's looking better. I thought we might have to amputate, but we managed to save your leg. You're lucky." He covered her up again.

Meilyr's expression turned serious. "You're doubly lucky, in fact. If Marc hadn't happened to stumble over you on his way back from a job, you would have died. Or, worse, the EAC would have found you."

"I was trying to get back here. I must have collapsed."

"Where were you when you were shot?"

"Near the orphanage."

"The orphanage you were investigating?! It's a miracle you made it this far with a wound like that. How come the person who shot you didn't finish you off?"

"I killed him." She swallowed. "Killed them all."

He frowned. "The best Crusader is a dead Crusader, but you might have created problems for us. When they find the bodies, they'll begin scouring the area looking for you. It's going to make things more dangerous for us."

"I'm sorry. I didn't intend to make your lives harder."

He nodded. "I know." He paused, appearing to weigh up what he was about to say. "I'm sorry you didn't find your children, Taylan, but now you've seen the situation first hand, I want you to think hard about what you're going to do next. Imagine if you *had* found your kids, could you have broken them out of the orphanage by yourself? And if you could have got them out, what about the ones you left behind? Don't you think they deserve freedom too?"

A painful lump swelled in her throat. "That isn't fair! Don't you think if I could help those children too, I would? I have to put my own family first."

"I'm just saying, the Occupation has affected everyone. If we all act solo, only looking out for ourselves, we'll never rid this island of the EAC. The Dwyr will win." He stood up. "I'll get you something to eat and drink. You need to build up your strength."

His words had sucked away all the relief and joy Taylan had felt after waking from her delirium. She'd been so happy to realize that seeing Dad, Kayla, and Patrin had been a fiction of her fevered, drugged mind. Her children weren't dead, or, at least, they could still be alive.

Meilyr didn't understand. Dwyr Orr knew what her children looked like. Taylan wasn't the only one trying to find them.

She tried to sit up, but her arms were too weak. How long had she been unconscious?

As she relaxed and stared at the ceiling, Meilyr's words continued to bite, and she thought about other things he'd mentioned, like how medical supplies were hard to come by. How much of their precious stores of antibiotics, painkillers, and sedatives had been used to save her?

A new face came into view: Meilyr's youngest brother, Marc. In the brief time she'd known him, he'd always been the friendliest and most easy going of the four siblings. He was smiling at her, his dark brown eyes twinkling.

"Glad you're back with us. It was touch and go for a while there."

"Meilyr said you found me and brought me here. You saved my life. I don't know how I'll ever—"

"It's not a big deal," he said. "No need to get all gushy. I'd do the same for any of us, and so would you." He sat on the stool and rested his forearms on the side of her bed. "Did you find out if your kids are at the orphanage?"

"I'm not sure, but I don't think they are. I watched the place for three days and didn't see them."

"What a shame. I'm sorry. Maybe they're at another one. There are twenty or so that we know of, dotted about. Most of them are in towns, though, which makes them harder to watch. I can find out their locations for you."

"I don't…"

"What?"

"I don't know if I should…" She paused, unable to go on.

"Taylan, what's wrong?"

She choked out, "Meilyr was saying I was being selfish, searching for my kids."

He gave her a look of disbelief. "I'm sure he didn't say that. Maybe you're still groggy from the drugs and misunderstood him."

"He didn't put it in those words, but it's what he meant. And he's right. I've used up your resources and time and done nothing to help the cause. But, Marc, it was because I wanted to help strangers that I lost them. If I hadn't handed them over to someone so I could help fight off the EAC, I would be with them today. I live with that decision every day, and every day it eats away at me."

"You don't know what might have happened if you hadn't handed them to someone else. If you hadn't help fight the Crusaders, you might all have died. It could be that because you chose to fight, they're alive today."

Taylan was unconvinced. She suspected he was only trying to make her feel better. "It isn't only that. The Dwyr knows I was the one who shot her in Jamaica and she has a vendetta against me. She also knows what my kids look like. She wants them too, and if she finds them before me, she'll use them to make me give myself up."

"Dwyr Orr is aboard the *Belladonna*," Marc replied. "I'm not saying that means your safe, but, considering all her resources, don't you think if she could find your children, she would have by now? I think they must be somewhere she can't get at them. Which means they aren't in a Crusader orphanage."

"The Dwyr still hasn't returned to her castle?" Taylan was relieved. She'd told Major Wright she might be able to spy on her for the Alliance, but so far all she'd done was try to find Kayla and Patrin.

"There's been no sight or sound of her or her weird new companion ever since the launch ceremony. Taylan, you have to do what you feel is best. No one here begrudges you anything, if that's what you're worried about. We all know what it's like to lose family."

You have to do what you feel is best.

Marc's words reminded her of what Arthur had said when he learned of her plan to desert from the Royal Marines. *You must do whatever you feel is right and just.*

What was the right thing to do?

Meilyr appeared at Marc's side. "It's just crackers and water," he said, "but I think that's probably all you can manage for now. Don't you have better things to do than bother our patient?" he asked his brother.

"I'm providing witty conversation to aid her recovery."

"Witty conversation? You? That'll be the day."

Marc winked at Taylan before leaving them.

"I-I thought about what you said," Taylan told Meilyr. She swallowed hard. What she was about to say hurt her almost more than she could bear. "When I'm better and up and about again, I'm going to do what I can to help the Resistance, for a while at least. I'm not giving up on my kids. I'm going to carry on trying to find out what happened to them, but, in the meantime, I'm yours."

"I'm glad to hear it. I'm sure we can use you."

14

———

The instant Wright stepped off the shuttle, Colbourn comm'd him. Wondering if she'd been watching a vidlink of the *Gallant's* bay, waiting to see him disembark, he replied, "Yes, Brigadier?"

"My office in two minutes, Major."

He winced at her harsh tone. Granted, she rarely softened it, but she had been known to on occasion, for him. Older officers had told him he'd been as close as anyone had ever come to being a favorite of hers. Now, since giving Ellis a compassionate discharge, all favoritism was out the window. He'd morphed into Colbourn's enemy number one.

He'd put her in an embarrassing, tricky situation by giving Ellis a discharge when he didn't have the authority. Neither did she, and she'd been forced to explain his actions to her CO. Though Wright didn't think embarrassment was the brigadier's problem. Her life philosophy was based on following the rules, and he'd flagrantly broken them. Maybe she'd thought he was the same as her, but she'd had a rude awakening. His version of the book included a human element she disregarded.

Squaring his shoulders, he set off through the unfamiliar

ship. He'd only spent a brief time aboard the *Gallant* before joining the counteroffensive in Jamaica and hadn't had time to learn her layout, though the Alliance's ships were all roughly the same.

The battlecruiser was a fairly new addition to the fleet. She had been held back from the attack on the *Bres*, though he wasn't sure why. It had been a lucky decision in the end because the *Gallant's* long-range scanners had picked up the *Fearless* out in the Asteroid Belt.

Now, both the *Fearless* and the *Valiant* were out of commission, undergoing repairs, and the Space Fleet bigwigs had picked the *Gallant* as their center of operations.

Pain lanced from his knee. He grimaced, stopped, and took a breather. His old wound had been bothering him all the time he'd been in Jamaica, and he'd run out of painkilling meds. For years, he'd put off getting the surgery that would fix it. There had always seemed to be something urgent and important that required his attention. Now, things were more hectic than ever. He guessed the surgery would have to wait until he retired, assuming he made it that far.

Colbourn's office door opened on an unexpected scene. Arthur and Merlin were sitting side by side across from Colbourn behind her desk. The two of them turned to him.

Arthur smiled. Merlin's expression was enigmatic, as always.

"Stop gawping and take a seat, Major," the brigadier snapped. "We don't have all day."

"Congratulations on your victory," said Arthur as Wright limped to one of two empty seats in the row of four. "I heard the battle was hard fought."

"Thanks, but I'm not responsible for the liberation of Jamaica."

"Not on your own, maybe, but I'm sure you fought valiantly."

"Can we save the standing ovation for Major Wright for another time?" asked Colbourn. Addressing him, she went on, "Do I have to ask you *again* to sit down?"

He lowered himself into the seat, wondering who the fourth was for.

"After your recent behavior," said Colbourn, "I argued long and hard against your inclusion in the operation we're about to discuss. Unfortunately, due to your history and unique position, I was given no choice." She paused, looking at him sourly. "I hope I don't need to impress upon you the importance of keeping the information you're about to learn to yourself?"

When Colbourn didn't like you, she really didn't hold back. He was insulted by the insinuation of distrust but only replied, "Of course not, Brigadier."

"If I might explain?" Merlin asked.

Colbourn's expression hardened further, but she nodded.

Turning to Wright, the alien said, "I've proposed another mission to strike at the heart of the EAC, and we need your help."

Ignoring Merlin, he asked Colbourn, "The Dwyr again?" It would be the Alliance's third attempt on her life.

"Yes."

"Brigadier, isn't this getting a bit old hat? We tried twice already, at the cost of many lives."

"Not that you're in any kind of position to be questioning orders," Colbourn seethed, "but the Alliance is in a precarious state. We barely managed to retake Jamaica, and now we're holding onto it by the skin of our teeth. The offensive in the Caribbean cost us heavily in personnel, armaments, and other infrastructure we will struggle to replace. If we can remove Dwyr Orr from the equation, it will bring the war to a swift end and *save* lives."

What she said made sense, but Wright had the weirdest impression from her words. It was like it wasn't really her speaking. As he paused, uncertain how to respond, Arthur spoke.

"You know Taylan well. We need you."

Ellis?!

"When we left the BI," Merlin said, "I was happy to leave Taylan there for the time being. I was unsure where Kala Orr would go. There was a chance she would return to her castle, in which case, Taylan's location was convenient. But the Dwyr has chosen to play it safe and remain on her flagship, the *Belladonna*. I was wondering how things would play out, waiting for the sign that would indicate which way to move, when I learned something significant about the *Gallant*."

Colbourn folded her arms over her chest. "The ship has a cloaking device," she interjected, in the tone of getting something out of the way. "A prototype the Space Fleet was fitting and testing prior to the Battle of the *Bres*. It's why the *Gallant* was held back."

"When Admiral Yorkson informed me of the ship's special capability," Merlin said, "everything slotted into place. The way forward became clear."

"Merlin proposes the *Gallant* approaches the *Belladonna* while cloaked," said Colbourn. "We board the ship, take over control, and kill the Dwyr."

"But, specifically, it must be Arthur or Taylan who assassinates the Dwyr," Merlin explained.

The brigadier rolled her eyes. "I don't think it matters, but who am I to—"

Her office door opened, and Lieutenant-General Carol entered.

Wright and Colbourn got to their feet and saluted.

"Brigadier, Major, at ease," said Carol, parking himself in the empty seat. "Where have you got to?"

"Major Wright knows the operation plan," Colbourn replied.

"Ah, good. It's a risky enterprise, I have to admit. But if we can succeed, it should put an end to the war entirely. I've always believed the fanaticism the Dwyr generates has been our greatest foe. Once she's out of the way, the EAC will fall apart. Most of her followers are ignorant and easily led. They just want something to believe in. If we remove the Dwyr and give them something more benign to latch onto...divine herbs or reading the future in compacted trash, something like that... our problems will disappear."

"Or someone else to believe in," said Merlin.

"Yes, perhaps we can give them another charismatic leader to follow. I know just the person." Carol patted Arthur's back. "But that's a discussion for another time. For now we need to focus on removing the Dwyr."

"If I might ask something..." said Wright.

"No need to stand on ceremony, Major," said Carol. "You have permission to speak freely."

"How is Taylan Ellis supposed to factor into this? She's no longer a Marine, and she's desperate to find her children. I doubt she'll agree to take part in a mission."

"She must," said Merlin. "Her presence is essential."

"Why?" Wright growled. "I know she's good—excellent, in fact—but we have plenty of—"

"She's *essential*," Merlin shot back.

The silence that followed was uncomfortable. No one would meet Wright's questioning gaze except Arthur, who, after a moment, said, "If Merlin says we need her, we need her, T.J."

The alien said, "I would explain—"

"Great," said Wright, "because I'd *love* to hear an explanation."

"But it would take far too long," Merlin concluded. "You'll have to trust me."

Wright snorted at the notion of having a smidgen of trust in him. "Rightly or wrongly, Taylan Ellis is discharged, She's a free agent. We can't compel her to do anything."

"That's where you come in, Major," said Carol. "Brigadier Colbourn informs me you have a special relationship with Ellis."

His eyes widening, Wright looked at the brigadier. She stared stonily back at him.

Did she think he'd discharged Ellis because they were hooking up?

"I'm sorry," he said to Carol acidly, "but you've been misinformed. My relationship with Taylan Ellis is, and has always been, entirely professional."

"Now, now," said the lieutenant-general, lifting his hands as if to forestall an argument, "I wasn't casting aspersions on your professionalism, Major. But you were her CO for most of her service, and you did act...shall we say, prematurely...in discharging her."

"The woman met the criteria," Wright retorted. "She's the only remaining parent to two young children. I don't know how she was even recruited in the first place. I guess the sergeant wanted to make his quota. Ellis *deserved* her discharge, and though I didn't go through the appropriate steps, it was because the situation didn't allow it. I've received a warning that's gone on my record, and that's it. The end. She's gone and she won't be coming back."

"Unfortunately," Carol said, "it isn't the end. We require her abilities again. Due to the unusual circumstances of her discharge, her comm implant wasn't removed, so we tried comming her, but—"

"She's in hostile territory!" exclaimed Wright. "The Crusaders could have picked up her location. You risked her life!"

"This was her reply," said Colbourn tersely, sliding an interface across the table.

He read the response, blanching a little at the cursing. He'd heard some rich language in his time in the Royal Marines. Ellis's was up there with the best of them.

"I'm not surprised," Wright said. "She probably guessed it's *him* who wants her back." He glared at Merlin. "The alien we've welcomed with open arms, not knowing what he is, where he's from, or why he's here."

"*Wright*," Colbourn warned.

"Brigadier," he replied, "Lieutenant-General, you know as well as I do the massive risk we're taking in allowing an unknown entity to influence the actions of the Britannic Alliance. It's madness."

"That's enough, Major," ordered Carol.

So he couldn't speak freely after all.

Merlin sat passively, expressionless. Arthur had his head down.

Wright clenched his jaw so tightly his teeth ground together. Colbourn *agreed* with him! He knew she did. Yet she wouldn't speak her mind in front of Carol or any of the other higher-ups. Something needed to be done about Merlin. He was hell bent on controlling the BA and eliminating Orr. Why? What did he care about human affairs?

"So that's why I'm here," Wright said dully, sudden weariness and a sense of powerlessness hitting him. "You want me to find Ellis and ask her to take part in the mission."

"Exactly," said Carol. "Communication with the West BI Resistance is sporadic and unreliable. The most recent report we had stated she'd left the group you met on your mission there. Then I asked the brigadier to try quickly comming her, with the result you've seen. We need someone to speak to her face to face, persuade her of the urgency and importance of the task we have in mind."

"She'll be searching for her children."

"Whatever she's doing," Carol said, "we need her to come back."

Wright sighed and shook his head. "And what if she's found them? You want me to ask her to abandon them again?"

"I'm sure she'll be able to find someone to leave them with while she's gone."

Wright looked into the lieutenant-general's eyes. The man's callousness was appalling.

"Look at it this way," Carol went on, "if she kills the Dwyr, the EAC will fall, her homeland will be free, and her children will be safe forever. Tell her that. I'm sure you'll be able to convince her."

"*If* I find her."

"I have every confidence in you," said Carol. He rose, saying, "Take twenty-four hours to recuperate before you set off. I'll leave the brigadier to brief you on the mission details."

After he'd left, tension hung in the air.

Wright felt trapped, almost as badly as he'd been at the barricade in Kingston. He couldn't imagine anything in the world he wanted to do less than attempt to drag Taylan Ellis away from trying to find her kids, unless it was to explain it was all Merlin's idea. Yet what could he do? The order came from the Lieutenant-General himself.

Eventually, he said, "If I'm to do this, I want to take Arthur with me." If he had to find Taylan, he could take the opportunity to remove Arthur from Merlin's influence. It was Arthur the Alliance leaders were in love with, based on his history. If he was physically separated from the alien, he might begin to understand Merlin was dangerous and he shouldn't go along with whatever he said.

"You aren't in a position to dictate conditions," said Colbourn icily.

"We can come to the BI with you," said Merlin, "if that's what you want."

"Not you, just Arthur."

"Out of the question," the alien said.

"Then I won't do it."

Colbourn's eyes blazed. "Are you refusing a direct order?!"

"I'll resign."

"You *know* that isn't how it works!"

Wright slammed her desk and leapt to his feet, reckless insanity racing in his veins. Feeling as though he was watching himself from a corner of the room, he said, "You want me to persuade Ellis to put her life in danger and risk leaving her kids orphaned in hostile territory. All on the whim of a goddamned alien! Something's up with you. Since when did *you* become *his* puppet?" He jabbed a finger in Merlin's direction.

"I don't want to do this," he went on through clenched teeth. "It's wrong! You know it's wrong too, but you're going along with it, just doing what you're told without question. Maybe it's about time we started questioning things, Brigadier!"

Colbourn stared at him for a cold, hard minute.

"Your request is granted. Arthur and only Arthur will accompany you."

Merlin shrugged.

"However," continued Colbourn, "before you set out, I want you to undertake a psych evaluation."

When Wright went to protest, she cut in, "That's an order, Major."

15

____

Lorcan pushed back his covers and climbed wearily out of bed. He'd been sleeping badly, and he didn't think he'd slept at all the previous night.

Despite the many years that had passed since he'd begun living permanently aboard the _Bres_, he still preferred to use the term 'night'. Naturally, there was no night or day on the ship or on her sisters, _Balor_ and _Banba_. Work on all three vessels continued round the clock. However, it was convenient to have the majority of his office and supervisory employees carrying out their duties at roughly the same time.

He looked up and left, activating a clock display in his vision.

Eleven-thirty AM?

He _had_ slept, after all.

Rubbing the sleep from his eyes, he padded to the bathroom.

The staff in the control center would be wondering what had happened to him. It was strange no one had checked on him. Or maybe they had and his implant had reported he was asleep. Or perhaps they hadn't, not caring whether he was okay.

He began his morning ablutions.

Things had changed since Iolani Hale had arrived. The atmosphere had lightened. He didn't like it. Building humanity's first colony ships was serious work. Leaving the Solar System and traveling to new, habitable planets was humankind's greatest endeavor. The names of the people who worked with him would go down in history along with his own, both on Earth and in the new civilizations they helped to found.

Their work was not supposed to be fun.

Didn't they understand the risks of losing concentration? The smallest error would be magnified thousands of times once the ships were underway. A little thoughtlessness, a simple mistake, could spell disaster for millions.

Despite Hale's shocking and harsh criticisms of the Project he had, on reflection, grown to somewhat appreciate her attempts to set them on a better path to success. But this new cheeriness, this conviviality, had to stop. She might know her stuff when it came to science, but he was the expert on workplace attitude and culture.

After the blower had dried him off, he got dressed, picked up a snack bar from the stash in his living room, and left for his two-minute commute.

When he reached the control center, the doors opened on a shocking scene.

No one was working. Rather than being hunched over their consoles as usual, his management team was standing around in small groups. What was worse, they were holding what looked like alcoholic drinks and were chatting to each other.

It beggared belief, but his staff had taken advantage of his unexpected absence and was holding a party!

"Lorcan." Iolani separated from a group and wove her way through the throng to join him. "I'm glad you decided to come."

"What..." he spluttered, hardly able to speak, "what the *hell* is going on?!"

"Didn't you get my message?" She was looking up at him, confused. Then she appeared to register his surprise and outrage. "You didn't. I see. Well, this is awkward. It's probably best I speak to you outside."

"You are not speaking to me outside or anywhere! Everyone, put down your drinks and get back to work immediately."

Hale's dogs suddenly bounded out from somewhere and loped over to Lorcan. After a cursory sniff, they stiffened, backed off, and softly growled, lifting their lips from their long teeth.

"Dogs in the workplace?!" Lorcan yelled, his voice lifting almost to a shriek. "Lock them up in your cabin now or I'll put them out the nearest airlock myself."

"You'll do no such thing!" Hale retorted. She signaled to the animals. They lay down on their stomachs, though neither took their eyes off Lorcan. "If you refuse to speak to me privately, I'll have to explain in front of everyone. Two valued colleagues of mine arrived this morning, and I was holding a short, informal gathering over an early lunch to welcome them and introduce them to the team."

"Without my permission?!"

"I sent you a comm at eight o'clock. You didn't read it. How was I to know you were going to have a lie in?"

"That's irrelevant. Why on Earth would you think holding a party on office time was appropriate or acceptable? Do you think I pay you to socialize and get pissed?"

"I just explained, we're taking an early—"

A man approached. Middle-aged with white hair and a pepper-and-salt beard, he had to be one of Hale's newly arrived colleagues.

"Ua Talman, I apologize for the mix up. If I'd known Iolani's reception would cause a problem, I wouldn't have agreed to it."

"It's fine, Anders," said Hale. "This isn't your fault." Her eyes narrowed as she looked at the person whose fault she clearly thought it was.

Quiet conversation had started up around them.

"Maybe it would be better if we continued this discussion elsewhere?" Anders suggested.

"But Lorcan insists we broadcast the misunderstanding to all and sundry," Iolani countered sarcastically.

"We can continue the discussion when my employees are back at their consoles and your dogs are safely locked up!"

Anders gave a small cough. "Iolani..." He looked at her, his expression pained.

"Oh, all right." She gestured at her dogs, who rose and trotted to her side. "This is for you, though," she said to her friend, "not *him.*"

As she was on her way out, Lorcan announced to the room, "Everyone back to work. The festivities are over. You will all make up the time lost today before you leave."

Groups of people began to disperse with soft grumbling and unfriendly glances in Lorcan's direction. He couldn't care less. He was their employer, not their friend. Over-familiarity with staff bred laziness and sloppiness.

"While we're here," said Anders, "might I introduce you to another of Iolani's friends who will be helping with the Project?"

"Please do," Lorcan replied. "Let's get the formalities out of the way."

The person in question was already walking toward them. This second unfamiliar face in his control center was more pleasant to Lorcan's eyes than the first. She was around the same age as Hale, though she couldn't look more different. She was almost as tall as him, her dark blonde hair was swept into a pleat at the back of her head, her features were even, and she moved delicately, like a doe.

Her smile was warm as she held out her hand. "Sorry about the kerfuffle. I'm Camilla Lebedev."

Lorcan felt soft skin and a firm grasp as he shook hands with her. "Apology accepted."

Now Hale was out of the way and everyone had returned to doing their jobs, he was calming down.

"Anders Kristiansen," said Anders, also shaking Lorcan's hand.

"I'm pleased to make both your acquaintances," Lorcan said. "Dr Lebedev, I've read some of your papers on human immunology, and Dr Kristiansen, I admire your work in genetics tremendously. I'm honored you agreed to come here, and I'm grateful you've agreed to spend your precious time working on my Project. I only wish our introduction could have been under more favorable circumstances."

"Let's pretend it never happened," said Camilla amiably.

Lorcan was finding it hard to take his eyes off of her. He'd seen vids of Camilla Lebedev at various talks and on media panels, but meeting her in the flesh, she looked different.

Suddenly, he realized what it was about her appearance that was striking him so forcibly.

She reminded him of Grace.

"Iolani has helped set up laboratories for you," he said, dragging himself back to the present. "Would you like to see them?"

"I would," said Camilla. "How about you, Anders?"

"To be honest, I was already tired after the shuttle flight and socializing at short notice has squeezed out the last of my energy. If it's okay with you, Lorcan, I'd like to take a couple of hours to rest and recuperate."

"Of course," Lorcan replied. "Take the rest of the day off and tomorrow too if you need it. I grant you it might not seem like it after what's happened, but I'm no slave driver."

"I never thought you were. See you tomorrow, Camilla."

Lorcan led his new employee through the *Bres's* passageways, taking his time, enjoying the pleasant sense of familiarity about her.

"Have you lived aboard a starship before?" he asked. "I know it isn't safe to spend much time in space anymore, but scientific research vessels used to be quite common."

"Sadly, no. I was offered the opportunity, but I always had something else to do that was either more urgent or more interesting. This will be a first for me."

"Then I'm doubly grateful you agreed to come."

"Iolani is an old, good friend who never asks for favors. It would have felt churlish to turn her down, but I'm also intrigued by what you're attempting here. And, I have to confess, funding is getting harder to come by every year. The prospect of not having to beg for every penny was appealing. How about you? How do you cope with living out here?"

"I enjoy it. The *Bres* has everything I need, including green spaces now that several habitats are up and running. Plus, I have to admit I'm a workaholic. If I spend too much time away from the Project, I begin to twitch." He did a bad impression of a nervous tic.

Camilla laughed. "I'm sure you don't, though I empathize with being a workaholic." She went on, "But, don't you feel out of touch with what's happening on Earth?"

"I've had my fill of Earth affairs. So much so, I'm spending trillions just to get away from them."

"Hmm, I feel like that sometimes myself. I take it you haven't heard the latest, then?"

Lorcan doubted any news he'd missed would interest him. Nevertheless, he replied, "I don't think so."

"The Britannic Alliance is said to have recovered an ancient artifact that will help them in their war with the EAC."

"An ancient artifact? That sounds like something more up the Dwyr's street."

"I know, right? I thought I must have misunderstood when I first heard about it, but it belongs to the Alliance."

"What is this thing exactly?"

"No one knows. Whatever it is, Dwyr Orr is so scared of it, she's fled to space."

Admiral Bujold had reported the woman was aboard the *Belladonna*, though he hadn't given the fact much thought. As long as the Crusaders stayed away from his precious ships, he didn't care what the madwoman did.

Iolani Hale marched up to them.

"I thought you might be on your way to the labs. I've 'locked my dogs up', as you put it, but I'm warning you, things are going to change around here, whether you like it or not."

16

———

Wright eyed the gigantic sword Arthur was insisting on bringing along on their trip to find Taylan Ellis. Only he and Arthur were in the cabin. Merlin was nowhere to be seen.

"Do you want a closer look?" Arthur asked.

The sword was enclosed in a plain scabbard printed on the *Gallant*, which was attached to a belt around the king's waist. The weapon stood out painfully, and Wright wondered how on Earth they were going to remain inconspicuous with Arthur carrying it wherever they went.

"Sure," he replied.

Arthur drew it out and gently grasped the blade so he could hand it to Wright hilt first. "Take care. It's very sharp."

He took it. He'd trained with knives for hand-to-hand combat, but he was out of practice, and in truth he wasn't comfortable with anything bigger than a steak knife. Most of his engagements involved killing at a distance.

The sword was surprisingly light for its size. As Arthur had warned, the edges were very fine and sharp. The solid section of blade ended about thirty centimeters from the tip. From

there, a groove ran down the center on both sides to the hilt—
to channel away blood, Wright guessed, a little nauseated.

The hilt was a wonder of craftsmanship, reminding him of the torc Arthur wore around his neck. Two slim dragons writhed from the guard to the grip, their legs forming the guard and their bodies entwining to create the grip. The pommel was a lion's head, fangs bared.

He examined the metal. It looked like regular steel. He didn't know much about the history of sword making, but he guessed that in Arthur's time the craft hadn't developed to creating ironwork of this caliber.

"Are you sure this is the same sword you used in your former life?" he asked. He wondered if Merlin had returned to the little church in the intervening centuries and replaced it with a more advanced model.

Arthur smiled politely as if the question was dumb. "I am sure."

"Where did you get it?"

This question conjured a bigger smile. "You wouldn't believe me if I told you, but, in short, a lady gave it to me."

"She must have been a helluva blacksmith."

"She was neither a blacksmith nor a swordsmith. Women didn't do that kind of work in my time."

Wright guessed Ellis probably knew the story of how Arthur got his sword. She was a fountain of knowledge on the subject of Arthur and his table of knights, or whatever it was.

He gave the sword back. "It's not what I'm used to, but I have to admit it's a beautiful weapon."

"It's strange," Arthur mused as he took it. "I didn't know Merlin had sealed Caledfwlch away along with my armor. I gave it to one of my knights to return to the lady who had given it to me. But I'm glad he took it. I don't feel complete without it." He slid the blade into its sheath.

Wright wasn't surprised Arthur had given his sword a name,

though he didn't quite catch what he'd called it. He also wasn't surprised he was so attached to it. When your weapon was the only thing standing between life and death, you tended to start seeing it as a personal friend. A lot of Marines got attached to their pulse rifles.

"I understand how much it means to you," he said, "but once we're planetside carrying that around is going to make life difficult for us."

"T.J., you made strong demands before you would agree to go to find Taylan. Bringing Caledfwlch with me is my demand."

"All right. I get it."

Merlin arrived, looking surprisingly chipper. Wright had expected him to make a bigger objection to being left behind, but he didn't seem to care.

"Are you leaving soon?" he asked.

"The dropship pilot is waiting for us right now," replied Wright.

"Then let me wish you a safe journey and a successful mission. I have a feeling you will find Taylan Ellis without too much difficulty."

"Is that so? Have you been *reading the signs*?"

"For someone who has no idea what they're talking about you're very scornful."

"I'd have a better idea if a certain person didn't play their cards so close to their chest."

"Knowledge is a precious thing," said Merlin. "You're right to desire it. Unfortunately, some things are beyond human beings' understanding. You'll have to...how should I put it?... trust me on this."

Arthur interjected, "I have everything I need, Major. We shouldn't keep the pilot waiting."

Ever the diplomat, the king was trying to head off the impending argument, but Wright wasn't about to have it out with Merlin anyway. Attempting to get information out of the creature was a pointless exercise.

Yet he couldn't help saying as he and Arthur left, "Trust is earned, Merlin, and you haven't done anything to earn mine yet."

~

THEIR ROUTE to West BI was to be the same as the one they'd taken when they'd attempted to assassinate the Dwyr. The dropship pilot would take them to Ireland, and then they would cross the Irish Sea by boat. They would make their way inland on foot, beginning their search for Ellis at the hideout in the Preseli Hills.

As he undertook the first part of their journey with Arthur, the only passengers aboard the small vessel, he hoped it wouldn't take them long to find her. They couldn't survive in hostile territory indefinitely. The longer they were there, the greater were their chances of being discovered by Crusaders, especially with Arthur carrying a massive sword.

But Ellis had said the king was impervious to pulse rounds. After witnessing his transformation from mummy to living, breathing human being, anything was possible. Ellis had also told him Arthur had turned into a killing machine at the invasion launch ceremony. That sounded far-fetched, but then so had her explanation of who Arthur was, and that had turned out to be true. He didn't know what to make of it all. Maybe if they were captured, the Dwyr couldn't hurt Arthur. The same couldn't be said for himself.

Now that Arthur was away from Merlin for the first time since the alien had coalesced from a cloud on the hull of the *Fearless*, Wright was eager to take the opportunity to probe him for information. His first question had been plaguing him ever since the meeting where he'd been assigned the mission.

"Arthur, do you know why Merlin wants Taylan so badly for this attack on the Dwyr?"

"When I was king, I had many knights to defend my kingdom, dispense justice, and maintain order. One of these was a very special man. A perfect knight in all ways except one."

An expression of pain and sorrow twisted the man's features. Wright wondered what the perfect knight's flaw had been. Whatever it was, it had left a deep wound.

After a pause, he went on, "No man could stand against him in battle, and in all knightly tests he was unbeaten. I don't know what happened to him after my final battle, but I doubt he was killed. What I do know is, at some point in his life, he must have fathered a child."

"Because you think Taylan is his descendant." As soon as Arthur had mentioned the knight's prowess Wright had put two and two together. "That's what Merlin told you? But how would that work over thousands of years, hundreds of generations?"

Arthur looked mildly annoyed.

"Sorry, but it's hard to believe your knight's abilities could be passed on so purely down the centuries."

"It isn't as simple as you think," said Arthur. "Anything involving Morgan le Fay or Merlin is extraordinary. My fate is tied up with the two of them, and my guess is, so is Taylan's."

"Are you saying Merlin had an influence on her abilities?"

"He may have, not directly, but through her ancestor. Our friend's fighting skills are not just unusually good, they're uncanny. It wouldn't surprise me if Merlin had something to do with them."

"He didn't tell you?"

"Merlin only reveals his secrets when it's useful to him."

"You can say that again! But I thought you and he were close."

"We are. But he is still his own man."

He isn't a man at all. But how to explain that to someone who only just found out the Earth orbits the Sun?

"Does Taylan know about her ancestry?"

"If she does, it isn't through me. I didn't know about it until Merlin identified her when we sparred with staves. After that, I didn't have an opportunity to explain it to her."

"Arthur, can you tell me something? Why do you put so much faith in Merlin? Do you think he has your best interests at heart?"

"I understand why you're suspicious. Many people of my time were suspicious of Merlin too. Some believed he was the Devil's progeny. But before I became king my country was a terrible, lawless place. Barbarous tribes raided the coastal areas or stole land and livestock and tried to settle. During my kingship, with Merlin's help, I put an end to all that. It became safe for ordinary people to travel through the forests, for families to farm their land without fear of enemies burning their crops, raping the women, and stealing children. By the time my challenger rose up against me, my kingdom was a peaceful, prosperous place. I could not have managed it without Merlin. I know he's easy to dislike, but I believe he has my and your interests at heart in all he does."

Wright didn't agree. From what he'd seen, the alien's motives were obscure, though now he could see better why Arthur stuck with him.

"Why do you think he kept you alive all these years?" he asked. "Why not find another Arthur to make king?"

"I'm not certain. Maybe he needs me in particular, or maybe it pleases him. He's hard to understand."

"Major Wright," said Colbourn via comm.

After asking Arthur to excuse him for a moment, he replied, "Yes, Brigadier?"

"I thought I should let you know, we've lost Merlin."

"*Lost* him?"

"Not long after you left, I tried to find him to discuss...you know. He couldn't be found. Lieutenant-General Carol ordered a shipwide search. He isn't anywhere on the *Gallant*."

"Could he have stowed away on a shuttle?"

"Yours is the only ship to depart since the last time he was seen, and as we both know, he doesn't need a ship to survive space."

17

———

"It'll take at least a week to get there," said Meilyr. "We should allow at least ten days in case of hold ups. Preferably two weeks." He sat at a table with his brothers. The four men huddled in as they discussed the next act of resistance against the Crusaders.

"Four weeks, there and back. It's a long time to spend in the wild," his brother, Madog, cautioned. "Every day we're out there increases our chances of being picked up."

"Are we any safer here?" asked Marc. "They're bound to find this place sooner or later."

Medwyn, the fourth brother, said, "I've been saying the same thing for months. We should move around regularly, not stay in one hideout all the time."

"If you know of anywhere else we could go," said Madog, "I'd love to hear it."

"*If* we could stick to discussing the plan..." Meilyr said, glaring from face to face.

Medwyn lifted his hands appeasingly. "I'm only saying..."

"Meilyr's right," said Madog. "We can decide whether to

move to another hideout when we get back...in about three weeks to a month?" He addressed the last comment to Meilyr.

"Midsummer is in two weeks," Meilyr replied. "The festivities are going to peak then. I'd feel happier if we set out tomorrow to be sure we don't miss it."

Taylan had been hearing snippets about the brothers' planned trip to Ynys Mon for several days, but she hadn't been included in the discussions. "I want to come too," she interjected, walking over to the group of men.

Meilyr looked up. "No, you aren't healed properly yet."

"I'm a lot better, and the exercise will do me good."

"We're talking thirty kilometers a day over hilly ground," said Madog. "That's not a little light physiotherapy."

"I can manage," Taylan protested. "I'm from around here, remember? You think I'm not used to hills?"

"No one's saying you don't know what you're talking about," said Marc.

"I am," said Medwyn, addressing the others. "We can't afford to take along anyone who isn't in good shape. What if she can't keep up or get under cover quickly if we see a patrol?"

"Hey!" Taylan exclaimed. "I'm right here. If you have an objection, say it to my face."

But he only scowled and refused to look at her.

"Medwyn has a point," Meilyr said. "This is going to be a tough mission. You might feel okay now, but what about after three or four days on the road? I know you want to help, but you could be a liability."

"If I start to slow you down, I'll turn back."

"And what if you're seen and put the EAC on our trail?" Medwyn asked.

"Now you're being ridiculous. Are you going to insist every member of the Resistance doesn't leave the hideout all the time you're gone?"

"No, but—"

"I trained and operated as a Royal Marine," said Taylan. "I have to admit sometimes I wasn't the best Marine in the world, but I still know more about military assaults than the four of you put together. You'd be idiots to not take me along."

"We'd be idiots if we took a cripple with us," Medwyn said, just loud enough to be heard.

Meilyr said, "Brother, your mouth has got you into trouble more than once. Keep running it and you'll be the one left behind."

Taylan felt bad for coming between the siblings. It was true, she wasn't a hundred percent fit yet, but her wound was nearly healed and only hurt at night or when she wasn't distracted. She was confident that in a week or so she'd be back to normal. However, by then the brothers would be halfway to Ynys Mon and the Crusaders' midsummer festival they intended to target.

"I'll leave you to decide," she said. "I can't make you take me, but if you do I think I can help."

She went to the corner of the underground chamber, where a makeshift kitchen had been set up. It wasn't much, just a stove that ran on batteries and a collection of battered pots and pans. An older man called David was the cook. He couldn't get around very well anymore, so his contribution to the cause consisted of creating meals from whatever supplies the fighters managed to steal and generally keeping the place clean and organized. He was about the only person who cared about the living conditions. Most of the rest of the group were—it had to be said—complete slobs.

He was leaning over the stove, stirring something in a pot, and didn't notice Taylan approach. When she reached his side, he jumped a little and the spoon banged against the side of the pan. He seemed alarmed. "What do you want? Dinner won't be ready for another half an hour."

"I thought you might need some help."

"No, no. No need. Go and relax."

"I don't want to relax. I'm bored. There has to be something I can do."

She was puzzled. She'd spent most of the previous afternoon helping David in the kitchen. He'd seemed grateful. Now, for some reason, his attitude toward her had done an about-face.

His shoulders slumped. "All right. How about you stir this for me while I try to find the salt? I made the mistake of leaving it out after yesterday's meal and now it's gone walkabout."

She took the spoon from him and peered into the big pot. He was making a stew of mostly root vegetables and beans. She tasted a little and grimaced. It did need salt, but also something else. While David was doddering around the room, she peeked into the boxes of dried ingredients on the shelf next to the cooker.

There it was.

The date on the box was the previous year, but this was the kind of thing that didn't go off. Its flavor only lessened over time. She opened up the box, finding it surprisingly full. She used to use this in her cooking all the time.

But just as she was about to add the dried fibers to the stew, a hand fastened on her arm.

"What do you think you're doing?" asked David, peering into the box.

He read the label. "Horseradish? What makes you think my stew needs horseradish?"

"I thought it could do with pepping up a little."

"Hand it over." He beckoned with his fingers.

Taylan hesitated, the dried horseradish fibers poised to be dropped into the pot.

"Hand it over," repeated David, "and step away from the stove."

"But..."

He stared at her with hard eyes.

Holding his gaze, she silently pushed the horseradish into the box and closed the lid. She gave it to him.

"Did you find the salt?" she asked.

"Yes, thank you."

He returned the box to the shelf and moved between her and the cooking pot so that she found herself looking at his back.

Dismissed by his body language, Taylan disconsolately went to sit in the place where she slept.

"Taylan," said Meilyr, noticing her, "we discussed your participation in the mission. We decided you're welcome to come, if you're sure that's what you want."

"I am, and I will. Thanks, guys."

Medwyn's expression was cloudy and he wouldn't look at her. She wondered if the brothers had taken a vote and it had been three to one.

"Grub's up," David announced. "Clear the table."

"Great," said Meilyr, leaning back. "I'm starving." Then a look of concern, almost fear, came over his features. He glanced from the kitchen area to Taylan, as if twigging she'd just come from there. "Did...did Taylan help to cook it?"

The four men shared expressions of alarm.

"No, she didn't," David replied. "This is entirely my own work. No *additional ingredients*."

"Phew," said Marc, visibly relaxing. "Dish it up then."

18

After several days of trekking across the West BI countryside, Wright and Arthur had stopped for the night in an abandoned farmhouse. The area near Dwyr Orr's castle was being closely watched, so they'd been forced to land much farther north and make their way cross country to the Preseli hideout. He doubted Taylan was still there, but it would be a starting point in their search. The fighters would probably know where she'd gone next.

The crossing from Ireland had gone smoothly, but getting out of West BI was going to be harder than entering it. He hadn't been able to give their Irish helpers a firm date for their return.

Spending time with Arthur had been an education. In his years of military service, Wright had met countless men and women from different cultures and backgrounds, but they all shared one similarity: they were of this time. Arthur was not. Wright found it hard to articulate his impression, even to himself, but it was as if the king saw reality in an entirely different way.

For one thing, he was deeply religious. Every night, before

going to sleep, he would get down on his knees, bow his head, and clasp his hands in prayer. And the man's religiosity extended much further than regularly praying. He seemed to see evidence of his beliefs all around him. Once, when they were nearly out of water, they'd happened upon a stream, and Arthur saw it as a sign that God was helping them. Another time, when they got lost, the ancient king was sure an evil spirit was leading them astray.

It was like he was living in another world.

Another interesting thing about him was his expertise at living in the wild. He could forecast rain hours before it arrived, and he seemed to have an instinctive sense of direction. Even when it was cloudy and they hadn't seen the sun or stars for days, he knew where the points of the compass lay. When asked how he was so certain, he said he just knew, and he was surprised that Wright didn't. Possibly, he was subconsciously reading the landscape or other signs, perhaps something he'd been taught as a child and internalized.

Arthur also spotted animal trails where Wright only saw ground cover or undergrowth, and he had a—it seemed to Wright—somewhat unhealthy obsession with their droppings. He could tell what animal had left them and how long ago. Given free rein, Wright was sure he would have set off to hunt them. He didn't like to eat the dry rations they'd brought along.

One thing Wright knew—accompanying Arthur was a re-education on everything he saw around him. If the sky was clear at night, the king explained the constellations he saw and the stories behind them. In the forests, he knew the name of every tree and the various uses of their wood.

The king's ease of existence within the natural landscape was surprising. Poor King Frederick, who had only reigned a few weeks before Dwyr Orr had murdered him, probably wouldn't have had the first idea about anything that existed beyond the walls of his palatial homes. Arthur had been royalty too, but perhaps his beginnings had been more humble.

"Goodnight," said the king, settling into his sleeping bag.

"Goodnight. You're sure if we make good speed tomorrow, we should reach the Preseli Hills by sunset?"

"Yes, that's my estimation. I hope we find Taylan there."

"Me too."

Wright fell asleep quickly, but, seemingly only minutes later, he was awake again. In the darkness, it was hard to tell how much time had passed. Arthur's heavy breathing indicated he hadn't woken. Wright wondered what had pulled him from his slumber. Normally, he would only be irritated—he hated being woken up—but in enemy territory, he had greater cause for concern.

He listened.

Raindrops pattered on the rickety farmhouse roof and the old concrete of the yard. He couldn't hear anything else, and nothing seemed to be moving within his field of vision.

Or was it?

He was facing the doorless opening to the outside. An empty window stood on each side of it. All three revealed nothing but the deepest night. Then he heard a very slight variation in the steady drumming of the rain, a regular sound, like...

He reached for the beamer he'd placed under the folded sweater he was using as a pillow.

"Arthur!" he hissed, wishing he was close enough to poke the man with his foot.

The king slept on.

He was sure he'd heard footsteps. Someone, either EAC or a member of the Resistance, was slowly creeping up on them. As far as he could tell, it was only one person, so naturally he or she was being cautious.

"Arthur!"

Nothing.

He lifted the beamer and aimed it at the doorway.

A figure separated from the darkness and stepped inside.

Wright rose onto his elbow and tried to press the trigger, but suddenly his intention to fire faded away and he wondered why he was holding a weapon.

"You can shoot me if you like, Major Wright, but I'm warning you, it won't have any effect."

"Merlin," Wright said angrily. "I was wondering when you would turn up."

"Thank you for the warm reception."

"I thought I'd made it clear I didn't want you around. If you insist on coming with us, I'm out. You can forget all about attacking the Dwyr's ship."

Arthur was rousing. "My old friend. You've come to help us find Taylan?"

"Exactly right. I don't think you'll manage it without me."

"We're *not* going to be managing it with you," retorted Wright.

"You might not understand it yet," said the alien, "but you need me. I would explain, but—"

"I wouldn't understand. Yeah, I get it. I don't care." Wright sat up to better address the shadowy figure in the dark. "You either let us do this on our own, or the deal's off. You might have pulled the wool over the Alliance's eyes, but not mine. I know there's a lot more to this than you're telling us, and you're not going to use me to achieve your aims. And if you think Ellis is more likely to agree to your scheme with you around to persuade her, you aren't the all-knowing, superior extra-terrestrial being you make yourself out to be. She doesn't trust you any more than I do."

"Perhaps you know her feelings better than I," Merlin conceded. "But you don't have the slightest idea what's happening here. These events are beyond human comprehension, and if you value the future of your planet, you would be wise to listen to me."

"Merlin has always been a faithful and trustworthy guide," Arthur gently interjected. "I've known him a long time, and he helped me greatly in my former life."

Wright ignored him. What Arthur was saying might be true, but it applied to the world of three and a half thousand years ago, not today. "What do you mean, *beyond human comprehension*? Try this human, then we'll see."

The whites of the alien's eyes were barely visible as he held Wright's gaze before appearing to come to a decision. He sat on the cold flagstones and crossed his legs.

"Earth is one of the very few planets in this galaxy inhabited by an intelligent species. There are...powers...who care very much what happens here. Over the history of your world, tens of thousands of conflicts have taken place. In Arthur's time, there were hundreds of controlling factions. Now, three organizations battle to decide Earth's fate. The Antarctic Project would like to see her stripped of resources and abandoned; the Earth Awareness Crusade want to return her to a state where traditional science is rejected in favor of a less...um...reliable understanding of the physical universe; the Britannic Alliance wants to remain on the current path of progress toward a better, safer, fairer civilization. The powers I represent support the Alliance's stance. I'm here to help it fulfill its aims. Is that explanation enough for you?"

"No."

Merlin had mostly told Wright what he already knew, except the part about the 'powers' and his role. That was not at all difficult to understand, so either the alien's comment about *events beyond human comprehension* was bullshit, or he was feeding him a line.

"Why do we need you to find Ellis?" he asked. "What do you know that we don't, and how do you know it?"

The alien smiled. For the first time since Wright had known him, the smile reached his eyes.

"Just as there are powers humans know nothing about, there are universal laws and patterns that shape all our destinies. Many of them even *I* cannot grasp, but I can read the signs of their operation. Don't bother asking for more details. No human language has the capacity to express what I mean."

"Why haven't you told the Alliance all this?"

"I prefer to rely on Arthur's legend to convince them of my usefulness. It's simpler, and, as you have said, the notion of an alien civilization exerting control over human affairs is...disconcerting?"

"Well, the cat's out of the bag now, isn't it? As soon as it's safe to comm Colbourn, I'll tell her everything you've said."

"I'll deny it. Who will they believe, I wonder? I read your psych assessment report."

He smiled again.

Wright's stomach plummeted. The assessment had gone badly. He'd recounted everything that had happened in the counteroffensive in Jamaica, and he'd lost it. He'd been surprised Colbourn had allowed him to continue with the mission to find Ellis, but he guessed Merlin had probably insisted.

Arthur said, "Would you agree to Merlin helping us to find Taylan, and then you and I talk to her?"

He wanted to say no. He wanted nothing to do with the creep, least of all introducing him back into Taylan's life. He'd feel like he betrayed her. But he couldn't see a way out of the situation. The only other option open to him was to desert, and he wasn't there yet. "I'll sleep on it."

As Wright lay on the hard floor, the sound of rain drumming in his ears, he recalled intending to shoot Merlin and the impulse inexplicably fading away. What had *that* been about? There was so much more to the alien than met the eye.

19

"You told me once that time doesn't exist," said Kala. "Can you explain what you mean? Each minute, hour, and day follows on from the one before, the planets circle their suns, and the Milky Way circles its center. How is it possible that time isn't real? I age, as all living things do, but I've noticed you do not. Do you exist outside of time?"

It was one of her regular learning sessions with Morgan. Her days aboard the *Belladonna* had fallen into a rhythm. She spent the mornings with Perran, teaching him the beliefs of the Crusade, and in the afternoons she became the student. Her classes took place in one of the flagship's briefing rooms so Morgan could use the holo display for visual illustrations. She was a fickle tutor, however. She flicked from subject to subject, quickly becoming bored and moving on, often before Kala truly grasped the relevant skill or knowledge. It was extremely frustrating, but if she complained, Morgan would make a veiled threat of some kind, usually involving Perran.

Her question to Morgan had been sparked by a message from one of her seneschals in the BI. Midsummer was drawing near, a significant date in the Crusade's calendar, and celebrations would be taking place all over the Isles as well as the rest of her realm. The message had been a respectful inquiry about whether she would be attending any of the festivities. The man wanted notice so that suitable preparations could be made, though he hadn't been so bold as to mention the fact.

She hadn't decided on her answer yet. Of all the momentous occasions of the year, she loved midsummer the best. The long day, heralding the warmth, vigor, and fecundity of the months to come, had a vitality and sense of abandon about it that she relished. In the years of her leadership of the Crusade, she'd never missed attending at least one celebration.

She was sorely tempted to return to Earth and indulge herself in some heady wantonness. The sterility of life aboard a starship didn't suit her. She longed for stormy nights, the crash of waves against rocks, the rush of wind through a forest. She also felt she was needed by her people. Her empire was slipping from her, and hiding away in space wasn't helping matters.

"Time exists for you in the sense that you perceive its passage," Morgan replied. "This is because in your experience cause and effect are irretrievably tied. In the same way, you're currently bound to the physical universe and subject to its laws and forces. I assume you're aware of the concept of time dilation?"

"Yes, I understand. After Ua Talman's ships launch, time will pass normally for the colonists, but from their perspective it will appear to speed up on Earth. A year on a ship could correspond to ten on Earth. And as the ships build up speed, time will appear to pass even faster on Earth. It means that if the colonists ever return, it will be to an Earth in the far distant future, a much longer duration will have passed than the time they have spent traveling."

"Good. Imagine an event on Earth, let's say, a volcanic eruption. On another planet, many light years distant, is another volcanic eruption. Do you agree that someone traveling in one of Ua Talman's ships would perceive the eruptions as happening at different moments than an observer on Earth would?"

"Yes, I can see that. The perspectives are different."

"And do you agree that each eruption has no relation to the other?"

"I suppose not."

"Well, it's also true that, at certain relative velocities, the person on the ship would observe the alien planet's eruption as occurring *prior* to the one on Earth. Separated events can appear in the future from one viewpoint and the past from another. Therefore, the ordering of events is not agreed upon by all observers. Therefore, all events that have happened and can happen are already in existence, in some sense."

"That's...remarkable," said Kala, trying to wrap her head around the concept.

"Your species' physicists already have this knowledge. I'm surprised you don't know it. Perhaps you should spend less time with your nose buried in dusty old books."

Kala had often had the impression that Morgan suspected her of reading the old stories where she appeared, and resented her for it. Or perhaps she feared Kala would stumble upon something she didn't want her to know.

"I prefer to spend my time learning high esoteric concepts," she replied haughtily, "not the mundane pontificating of scientists. They never raise their eyes from their research findings. Besides, you've shown me many times that their understanding is narrow and small-minded. Some things you can do, they say are impossible. Telepathy, for instance."

"Telepathy *is* impossible for most humans, or, at least, very difficult."

"So I can only do it because I'm related to you?"

"I think saying you can 'do it' is an exaggeration of your capabilities..."

Beneath the table they were sitting at, Kala clenched her hands into fists so tightly her nails dug painfully into her palms. Morgan's insults were outrageous and intolerable. Whenever she threw out one of her cutting remarks, Kala's resolution to kill her grew stronger. If only she knew how to do it. Morgan had arrived at the *Belladonna* under her own steam, not requiring a shuttle to bring her, so putting her out an airlock would be useless. That didn't stop Kala from imagining watching the woman gasping for air as her blood tried to force its way out of her body.

"... practice will help you retain your current level," Morgan was saying. Kala had missed her intervening words, but it had probably been more disrespect and obfuscation. As usual, her direct question hadn't received a direct answer. "Perran, on the other hand—"

"Perran is still very young," Kala interrupted, steering the focus away from her son. "Speaking of age, I noticed that you don't. Age, I mean. You haven't changed at all, not from the moment I first set eyes on you over thirty years ago. I was wondering, thinking over what you were saying about time, is that because its passage doesn't affect you? I ask you again, *do* you exist outside of time?"

Morgan's face took on a distinctly surprised look. Kala felt as though she was catching her off guard for the first time.

"What an extraordinary question!" she retorted. "Exist outside of time? How could I do that?"

The illusion faded. Morgan was not surprised at all. She was teasing her.

Kala's fingernails bit so deeply they broke skin. Before her fury burst out and she did or said something she would later regret, she rose stiffly to her feet and excused herself. Feeling Morgan's amused gaze on her back, she stalked from the room.

She would not tolerate the woman's disrespect any longer! She had to do something to put an end to her. Learning new skills and knowledge be damned. Nothing was worth the suffering Morgan inflicted on her or the threat she posed. She was always niggardly with her teachings anyway. A little telepathy here, some insight into the workings of the universe there. Never enough, every session unsatisfying. Kala suspected that what she'd interpreted as Morgan's short attention span was actually a deliberate ploy. She had never wanted her to learn anything properly. Rather, she was going behind her back to teach Perran everything thoroughly, shaping him to lead the Crusade. A young man would be easier to manipulate than herself.

As soon as Perran was ready, Morgan would find a way of getting rid of her. She was not entirely invulnerable. Arthur and Taylan Ellis could kill her. That was it. That was how she would do it. Morgan would engineer a scenario where Arthur or Ellis could reach her.

Well, Morgan had enemies too. She'd mentioned someone, though not his name. The person who had given Arthur and Taylan—by descent—the power to hurt her. Morgan feared him. Kala was sure of it. Was he the one who had imprisoned her thousands of years ago? Had he survived all this time as well?

She had to find out who it was and if he was still alive. Then, she would find him and persuade him to murder Morgan. Most likely, he wouldn't need much persuasion. Did he know she'd escaped her prison? He might be seeking her out right now, wanting to recapture her and return her to her lonely, cold, underground chambers.

Kala had more research to do, and for that she needed her books.

20

———

Suitable places in which to hold a meeting of Alliance and Jamaican representatives were few and far between. Every substantial building still standing in Kingston after the battle for control of the city was internally wrecked. The Ambassador's Residence stank of human waste, infected wounds, and death; the former seat of the temporary Parliament had been partially destroyed in the coup, even before Dwyr Orr's forces attacked; and the Crusaders had defiled the stately home they had commandeered for their seat of operations.

Hans had proposed they use the university. The EAC's distrust and dislike of conventional education had meant that, after capturing and killing any academics or students they could find, they'd left the place alone. The halls and lecture rooms had contained little in the way of food or regular, everyday items to attract looters.

How different the assembly was from the last General Council meeting before everything had gone to pot. The ranks of military officers in their uniforms, the MPs in their smart suits, poor Queen Alice in her regalia...they seemed dream-like to Hans, not actual memories of real people. And the splendid, ornate wooden hall where the meeting had been held was a fantasy compared to the stark, plain walls of the university's auditorium.

The new BA military heads, Chief of Defence Staff Evans and Sea Lord Fox, looked somewhat disheveled. Hans couldn't imagine Hennessy or Montague ever appearing less than perfectly dressed. He knew the fight for the Caribbean had been hard, but that was no excuse to allow standards to slip.

Other Alliance representatives, including the BA's Foreign Secretary and Defence Secretary looked smarter, but even their outfits were crumpled and seemed cheap, as if created by printer rather than human hands.

The Resistance leaders had more reason to appear rough and ready. Hans didn't know much about Devon's or Charles's or the other leaders' backgrounds, but he doubted any had held positions of power. They were good men and women—honest, brave, and principled—but they were not at ease with the etiquette of higher social echelons.

That was where he came in.

"Welcome to the first of what I hope will be many, and fruitful, discussions on the future of Jamaica," Hans said to the assembly. He'd persuaded the Resistance to allow him to guide the talks.

"Not too many, Jonte," joked the Foreign Secretary, Blake. "I think we don't have too much to discuss here, do we?"

Hans had thought all the BA Government reps were new to him, but he suddenly realized he knew Blake from his time as Head of SIS. He'd thought none of the government members living on the island had survived the invasion, but she clearly had.

What had been her role? He had a vague idea she'd been a junior minister in the Health Department. How on Earth had she risen to her current position so quickly? He guessed the sudden vacuum in the highest positions had sucked in all kinds of detritus from the lower ranks.

"I would say we have a great deal to discuss, Foreign Secretary," Hans replied.

He had a tricky course to steer. The Jamaicans thought he was entirely on their side, desiring complete self-governance for the island, while the BA knew he was playing a double game, that he would pretend to push for autonomy but in fact he supported the Alliance.

"I don't see why," said Blake. "We had a clear structure for the government of Jamaica and the rest of the Caribbean not so long ago. All we have to do is to return to the way things were. It's actually the rebuilding effort and other support the Alliance is prepared to offer that we're here to discuss, isn't it?"

"Exactly," said Defence Secretary Michaels, a man Hans didn't recognize at all. "As you might imagine," he went on, addressing the Resistance leaders, "our resources are extremely stretched at the moment. Naturally, we'll do everything in our power to help all we can. It's in all our best interests, after all. But it would be wise to prepare your followers for things to take much longer to return to normal than they might expect."

"Well," said Hans, pleased that Blake and Michaels were playing their parts effectively, "it's only fair that the Alliance should help Jamaica get to its feet again after so many years of exploitation of its people and siphoning off its most valuable assets, but perhaps it would also be wise to prepare yourselves for things to *not* return to how they were before the EAC invasion."

"I'm not sure what you mean," said Blake, in a low, menacing tone.

What a good actress she was.

"I mean, the cataclysmic disaster Jamaica has suffered is at least in part due to the Alliance's interference in its affairs. If the BA Government hadn't transferred here, the island would not have been so attractive to the Crusaders. A continued Alliance presence here is something we Jamaicans must think about carefully."

Sea Lord Fox snorted and said, "So 'you Jamaicans'..." making fun of Hans for ascribing the nationality to himself "... want to have your cake and eat it. You want us to front the cost of all the repair work and then hand over control of the territory to you, receiving nothing in return. This isn't the first hint I've heard in that vein, but it's the first time I've heard it proposed formally."

"How is it any different from what you did to us?" Charles growled. "How many of us fronted the cost of the Alliance with cheap labor and unfair trade practices? How long have you been draining the Caribbean in order to fund your royal palaces and dinner parties?"

"If you think the Alliance spends any more than a tiny percentage of its budget on the Royal Family," said Blake, "you're mistaken. Please educate yourself if you wish your opinions to be respected."

This attack caused an almost palpable shockwave of anger to pass through the Jamaicans. Hans heard the enraged murmurs and mentally scrambled to think of something to say that would calm the rising tensions.

"Before we can talk about budgets," he said, "we should figure out what's needed here. The Alliance has already restored the net, which is great, but many areas are still without power or running water. It's safe to say, if we don't have these basic necessities restored, we'll see a massive outbreak of disease within the next few weeks."

"Yes, yes," said Michaels irritably. "The Chief of Defence Staff has already allocated significant numbers of troops and sappers to repair power lines and water pipes. But we're stretched thinner than we've ever been. You can't expect miracles. And you can't expect the Alliance to devote precious resources to these projects without the resumption of control, which seems to be the sticking point. I'll have to speak directly to the Prime Minister about the matter, but after what I've heard today, I'll be pushing for legally binding assurances that Jamaica will return to being within the Alliance and the seat of the BA's temporary Parliament, until such time as it can return to the Britannic Isles. I think that's reasonable?"

He turned to the Alliance representatives for their support. Blake nodded vigorously and the military chiefs grunted their assent.

What was Michaels doing? The Jamaicans would never sign anything that would give up their country to the BA again.

"Let's not be hasty," said Hans. "The last few months have been devastating for the Caribbean and the Alliance. We all need time to reflect, take stock, and, after careful consideration, figure out a mutually agreeable way forward. Resorting to legal agreements is heavy-handed and unnecessary at this early stage. We need to focus on the people of the islands and averting the impending humanitarian crisis."

Didn't they understand from his message he had a handle on the situation and that he was going to work from within to bring Jamaica back into the fold? Surely these officials weren't so stupid they thought they could bully the locals into submission? He hadn't lived among them for long, but even he knew this was exactly the wrong tactic to employ. If they were pushed, they would push back, hard. Resentment and the desire for independence was strong.

"My men and women gave their lives for this country!" Evans burst out, speaking aloud for the first time. "I'll be damned if I see it leave the Alliance."

"Indeed," echoed Fox, leaning forward and glaring at the Jamaicans. "I'd advise you all to think carefully about biting the hand that's fed you up until now. It would be very unwise for a small, poor country to leave the protection of its benefactor.

You would also be weakening what's currently the only force for good in the world. How long do you think it would take Dwyr Orr to swoop in and finish you off after you boot us out, eh? How long will you survive your second dose of Crusader zeal?"

"Benefactor?" muttered Devon. Then, louder, he repeated, "Benefactor?! My parents slaved twelve hours a day in Alliance munitions plants that poisoned the air they breathed, the soil my grandparents farmed, and the seas we fish in. For what reward? Wages barely high enough to pay the rent and put food in our bellies. Do not talk to me about how we benefited from the Alliance. I'm done here!"

He stormed out. The other Resistance leaders were not slow to follow him. Within half a minute, only Hans was left, facing the stunned members of the Alliance.

"That went well," a junior official quipped.

"It went very badly," said Hans quietly, gritting his teeth. "Don't any of you understand this process has to be undertaken carefully?"

"What process?" asked Blake. "Moving Jamaica toward independence?"

"No! Returning the country to the Alliance."

"What are you blathering about?" asked Michaels. "What happened to our exploitation of the Jamaican people and siphoning off the country's resources?"

"I had to say that," Hans hissed, checking over his shoulder and hoping no Resistance leaders lingered outside the closed door to eavesdrop. "I have to—"

"Make up your mind, Jonte," said Blake dryly. "A moment ago you were Jamaican. When you decide which side you're on, let us know. For now, I think we need to step away, halt all work on rebuilding projects, and wait for legal assurances that Jamaica will remain an Alliance territory. Are we agreed?" She looked to her colleagues for their agreement.

"No, you mustn't do that," said Hans. "You'll ruin everything I've been working toward. Didn't you get my message?"

"I think you might have spent a little too much time in the sun, sir," said the junior minister, not unkindly. "Maybe you should get yourself checked over."

"Do it quickly, though," added Michaels. "Alliance medical support will be gone in a day or so. Now, who's for an early lunch? I'm famished."

Ignoring Hans's protests, the delegation filed out of the auditorium.

21

Things were changing on the *Bres*, as Hale had warned, but not in the way Lorcan had feared. The arrival of Camilla and Anders had injected a breath of fresh air into the place. He hadn't realized it until he noticed the change, but the atmosphere had grown monotonous and stale over the years.

He'd thought Hale's presence would encourage slacking off and insubordination. It would be hard for her to rein in her resentment of his earlier treatment of her. But she and her scientist friends were consummate professionals once they got their heads down, and their attitude prompted new vigor and attention to detail in Kekoa, Jurrah, Steadman, and the rest of the heads of departments.

He had a feeling the effect wasn't what Hale had meant, however, and he was waiting for the other shoe to drop.

In the meantime, he was enjoying the better working environment. He was particularly enjoying the presence of Camilla Lebedev. He'd made a habit of visiting her and Anders in their respective laboratories every day, learning about their disciplines and their ideas on how to solve the potential problems colonists might encounter on their new planet.

Camilla was trying to develop a drug that would suppress the human immune response to external stimuli but not affect the body's ability to detect and destroy anomalous cells of its own, that is, cancerous cells. Many treatments already existed, but she was working on one that could be easily synthesized from common, readily available substances.

Anders' work was more innovative. He was trying to create a protocell, a cell containing the basic components for self-sustaining life that could be genetically engineered into any number of different life forms. If the conditions on the colony planet were not suitable for farming any Earth plant or animal species, the protocell could be programmed to survive and reproduce in the existing conditions, perhaps as an algae, cereal crop, or even livestock. Because it wasn't native to the new world, the new life form would also be unlikely to provoke an allergic reaction in humans.

Though Anders work was more interesting to Lorcan, he found Camilla more interesting as a person. He'd chided himself for his foolishness over and over again, but he couldn't shake the impression of her similarity to Grace. What was even more affecting was the fact she was around the same age his wife had been when she'd died. That had been decades ago, and now, in comparison to her, he was an old man. And yet...

"Penny for them," said Camilla pleasantly, peering at figures on a screen.

"I'm sorry, what?" Lorcan replied, startled out of his reverie. He'd been hanging about in Camilla's lab for an hour or so, checking her latest results. He'd offered up his own blood and bone marrow for her to use, so he felt a personal involvement in her experiments. That was his excuse for being there, anyway, and he was sticking to it.

"Penny for your thoughts," she said. "Haven't you heard of that saying?"

"Only a penny? I suppose that seems a fair price for what passes through my head these days."

"What? Don't put yourself down. I'm sure the musings of the founder of the Antarctic Project must be worth a little more than that. Maybe a whole cred?"

He laughed. Then, instant guilt swept over him. What was he thinking? There had been a time he'd sworn he would never—

"Would you like to see something interesting?" Camilla asked.

"I'd love to. I hope you don't find my presence intrusive."

"Oh, no. It's nice to have some company. I heard there used to be a time when laboratories were filled with staff, all working together. But nowadays, so much of what I do is automated. It can get a little lonely."

She took a step away from the upright interface and swept an arm toward it, inviting him to take a look.

"As you know, your samples demonstrated you're allergic to grass pollen and shellfish."

"Yes."

"Look at this." Camilla pointed at a column of figures. "This is your immunoglobulin E response to those allergens. Now, compare those numbers to these." She pointed at a second column. The figures were all lower, including some zeros.

"You did it," said Lorcan. "You created an immunosuppressive treatment."

"I did." She smiled. "But don't get too excited. It isn't a groundbreaking achievement these days. I just swapped some of the rarer components for more widely available ones. I still have a lot of work to do. I have to replicate the results, test the treatment's safety, and then go on to develop it further. Then more testing. It'll be years before I'm finished."

"We have years," said Lorcan. "I mean, I have. I mean, the Project has. It'll be years before all the ships are ready." He was stumbling over his words, feeling like a fool.

"Lorcan, where are you?"

Iolani Hale was comming him.

"Excuse me," he said to Camilla before replying, "I'm in Dr Lebedev's lab. What do you want?"

"I want to speak to you. I'll be right there."

What Hale hadn't considered was whether Lorcan wanted to speak to *her*. But it appeared she was on her way regardless.

"Was that Iolani?" Camilla asked.

"Yes. She'll be here imminently."

"I thought you would be hearing from her soon. She's been looking into something that concerned her."

"Something to do with the ship?"

"No, something—"

The lab door opened, and Hale stomped in like a diminutive, grounded, avenging angel.

"I found it," she announced. "I finally found it. I always knew your operation was dirty. I just didn't know how dirty. Can I use this?" she asked Camilla, pointing at the interface.

"Go ahead."

Lorcan braced himself for another onslaught of Hale's animosity. Was she ever going to let up on delivering her endless streams of hatred? He got the point already. That was why she was here, interfering in everything he was doing.

She was searching for something.

"Look, whatever it is you think you have on me," he said, "I suggest you check your sources carefully. You might not agree with my methods, but everything that occurs under the umbrella of the Antarctic Project is legal and above board."

"Hmpf. Are you sure about that?" Hale replied, her attention not leaving the screen. "Dammit. Where's it gone? Ah, here it is. Take a look at *this*, Ua Talman, and then tell me how you sleep at night."

The display showed a vid of young miners emerging from a mine in what looked like a tropical country. He looked more closely. The miners looked very young. Too young.

His confidence withered.

"How do I know this isn't fake?" he protested. "Or that it's even one of my mines?" As he spoke, the sign at the front of the mine came into view. KAMBOTO MINE. Underneath the name was written: Subsidiary of the Antarctic Project.

"Child labor!" Hale spat. "You have *children* mining cobalt for you, in dangerous, inhumane conditions. Kids slaving away, getting sick, dying or living with lifelong disabilities so you can fulfill your ambitions. What do you have to say to *that*, Ua Talman?"

A pause dragged out. He'd genuinely had no idea what had been going on at the Kamboto Mine. But he didn't try to offer up the excuse. It was no excuse. He *should* have known.

"You used to have children, didn't you?" Hale asked.

"Stop."

"How would you feel if—"

"That's enough!"

"What I don't understand is—"

"You really are relentless, aren't you?" he growled.

She was speaking over him, saying, "why you even bother mining cobalt on Earth when there are asteroids rich in it and almost everything else you need. Why, Lorcan? Why?!"

He was already on his way to the door. He couldn't bear to hear another word.

22

They arrived at the Resistance hideout a couple of hours before dawn. The Preseli Hills were silent in the darkness. The sky was cloaked in thick clouds, from which a soft, blanketing rain was falling. Arthur had brought them unerringly and confidently to the correct place. He'd begun recognizing signs from several kilometers away, signs entirely invisible to Wright. To him, the rolling green hills and wooded valleys were attractively scenic but looked much the same.

He knew from the time he'd spent at the hideout that the fighters had adopted a nocturnal lifestyle, carrying out most of their activities at night, so he wasn't worried about surprising them while they were sleeping.

What he *was* worried about was being mistaken for a Crusader by the lookout and killed before anyone took the trouble to check.

If only Taylan were here. She could call out a few words of Welsh to the person stationed near the entrance, and they would probably be safe to approach, even though they didn't know that night's password.

Taylan could be here. Only *inside* the hideout.

"I know what you're thinking," whispered Merlin. He was standing behind Wright in the lee of the hill opposite, where they'd halted.

Wright's skin crawled at the alien's proximity. He took a step forward.

"I'll go forward first, with Arthur," Merlin continued.

"No." He didn't trust him in the slightest, and he had no idea what he might do if given free rein. Ellis was clearly important to him. According to Arthur, Merlin saw her as the king's second-in-command, or something like that. Or he could have other plans for her. Whatever his interest was, it wasn't to Taylan's benefit. That, Wright was sure of. The only interests important to the alien were his own.

So he wasn't going to let Merlin get to her first, assuming she was there.

"Then what's your plan, *Major*?"

The problem was, the EAC was looking for Taylan, so he couldn't shout out to the lookout that he was from the Alliance and he wanted to speak to her. That would be exactly what a Crusader would say. He could try telling the lookout who he was. He'd stayed at the hideout for a couple of days, but the person who he'd had the most dealings with, Angharad, was dead. There was a chance he wouldn't be believed, and by talking he would alert the lookout to their presence. He didn't want to fall victim to some terrified, trigger-happy youngster on duty for the first time.

"My plan is that you and Arthur wait here."

He would have to sneak up and disarm the man or woman. Then he could provide convincing reassurances without the risk of having his head blown off.

Dropping his pack to the ground, he stepped onto the track and began to return the way they'd come. He would have to leave the track and approach the hideout hill from the opposite direction to come at the lookout from behind.

Fifteen minutes later, after toiling over the rough stones of the hills, he was finally in position. The lookout was hiding in a cleft between two large, upright sandstone outcrops. The interior was entirely in shadow and just large enough for one person to sit comfortably. The spot commanded a wide view of the area before the hideout. No one could get within fifty meters of it without the lookout radioing a warning to those inside, then shooting to kill.

Wright crept forward, skirting the edge of one of the massive rocks. The rain had begun to come down hard, turning the slope into a wide, shallow stream.

Just as he was about to spring around the front of the boulder and leap on the person inside, he slipped on water-loosened scree and his legs went out from under him. Rather than grabbing and restraining the lookout, he found himself sprawling at his feet.

"Wait!" he yelled, lifting his hands, "I'm not a Crusader! I'm from the Alliance."

But the man either didn't hear, didn't understand Wright's English, or wasn't listening.

He attacked.

Wright deflected the blade aimed at his throat and grabbed the man's wrist. They were sliding down the slope, grappling in the loose shale. The lookout was on top of him. He fought to turn the man over, dodging the jabs of the knife that were coming at him despite his hold on the other's wrist.

He couldn't kill him, not even in self-defense. That would go down among the Resistance like one of the stone slabs that dotted the hills hereabout. He had to get him to stop fighting long enough to listen. The way the fight was going, however, Wright would count himself lucky to simply survive.

The knife plunged into the ground next to his head. And

stuck. As the man struggled to free it, Wright slid out from under him. He yelled again, "I'm Alliance, Alliance!"

Wrenching out the blade, the lookout swung at him. Wright ducked.

A dark figure appeared in the darkness, looming tall. Two large arms wrapped around the lookout, pinning his own to his sides, and lifted him until his feet left the ground.

The man began to yell in Welsh, no doubt trying to warn the Resistance members inside the hideout.

"It's okay!" Wright tried to reassure him. "Do you understand English? I'm Major Wright from the Britannic Alliance. I was here a few months ago."

It was no use. The man continued yelling. Within seconds, fighters were pouring out. Some were carrying pulse rifles.

"Stay where you are, T.J.," said Arthur. He stood between Wright and the hideout exit.

As he spoke, a pulse round hit his back.

He didn't react.

The energy washed over him like a wave splashing over a rock.

Wright gaped.

Ellis had told him Arthur was impervious to pulses, but he hadn't quite believed it. All his adult life he'd witnessed the devastating effects of the rounds and suffered them, too. Seeing Arthur unaffected by the bolt of energy was like seeing the sun rise in the west.

Above the shouts and yells came the sound of Merlin calling out. The reaction of the fighters stopped almost as soon as it had started. The lookout relaxed in Arthur's arms and tried to peer around him to see what was going on.

Someone replied to Merlin, who was walking toward the group from the opposite hill.

They understood him. He could speak Welsh, like Taylan. Of course he could. He'd also spoken English the moment he stepped aboard the *Fearless*. The alien hadn't needed the speed learning software Arthur had used. He knew English, Welsh, and probably every other language spoken on Earth, possibly every language that had ever been spoken on the planet.

Arthur put the lookout down. The man was clearly no longer any danger. He reached out to take Wright's hand and shook it, saying, "Sorry."

"No, I'm sorry for surprising you. I was trying to..."

But the man was already leaving them, going to join the group at the hideout entrance.

Merlin beckoned.

When Wright and Arthur joined him, he said, "They want us to go inside quickly, in case there are any Crusaders nearby."

The hideout hadn't changed at all from how Wright remembered it. Dark, dank, and smelling of unwashed clothes, the place was just as cramped and crowded. Another thing he noticed immediately was that Taylan wasn't here. She would have come over to him and Arthur right away if she was.

A few of the fighters were fluent in English, though the lookout was not at all. One of them translated for him when he said he was glad no one got hurt in their tussle.

"I'm glad too," Wright replied.

Merlin was, predictably, taking the lead, chattering away in the country's native tongue. Wright could only stand impotently by and wait the outcome of the discussion.

After a few minutes' talk, the alien turned to him and said, "She was here. She went to find her children, but she'd been shot by Crusaders—"

"Shot!"

"She made it back, and they treated her. She's better now, but she's gone again. A small group left ten days ago and she went with them. They're on their way to Bryn Celli Ddu."

"And where's that?"

"Ynys Mon."

Another place name Wright hadn't heard of and would struggle even to pronounce.

"Why are they going there?"

"Bryn Celli Ddu is a very ancient, very sacred place."

"They want to fuck up a Crusader festival."

"Exactly."

23

Despite the challenges waiting at the end of their journey, Taylan was enjoying her time with Angharad's sons. Their long treks under the stars or through cloudy, wet nights didn't hurt her leg too much, and she had plenty of time to recover during the day while they rested and slept.

At that time of year the nights were short and the days long, so in order to reach their destination by midsummer's eve, they had to leave an hour before sunset and halt an hour after sunrise. The potential exposure to unwanted observers was risky, but they had no choice.

After the sun rose, they would pick up pieces of fallen, dry wood until it was time to stop. By then, they usually had enough to build a hot, fast-burning fire that produced little smoke. The men would take turns at making cakes of stiff dough out of flour, oats, baking powder, salt, and water, which they cooked on stones placed on the edge of the fire. For some reason, Taylan was never asked to take a turn. They also foraged for food during the daylight hours to help eke out their rations, though little was available at that time of year. They picked honeysuckle flowers in woods, sucking out their sweet nectar. When they reached the coast, they ate the sea kale growing in the shingle. A kind of tea made from elderflowers relieved the monotony of drinking plain water.

Sixteen hours of daylight every day as the summer solstice approached was far too much time to spend sleeping. After waking, they would huddle in whatever shelter they'd managed to find and discuss plans to disrupt the festival the Crusaders were about to hold at Bryn Celli Ddu on Ynys Mon.

The tomb was so old no one knew who had built it. As the sun rose on midsummer morning, it would shine down the tomb's central passage and light up the interior, marking the beginning of the EAC's biggest annual celebration. Huge numbers of the Dwyr's followers would be gathered and out of their minds on alcohol and hallucinogens. It would be the perfect opportunity to do the movement some real damage.

One late afternoon, after they'd woken up and eaten and were waiting to set off for another night's walk, talk of sabotaging the midsummer festival had run dry.

Marc said, "Taylan, is it true the men who were with you when you first came to the Preseli Hills—not the Marines, the other ones—is it true they were King Arthur and Merlin?"

Before she could answer, Medwyn broke in, "I never heard such nonsense in all my life! Of course it's not true. Two wanderers who stole a sword and chainmail from a museum, that's all they were."

"Shut up," Marc told his brother. "I asked Taylan, not you."

The young man's eyes were shining with excitement. Taylan knew how he felt. She'd been just as excited when she'd realized King Arthur had returned to save the BI, exactly as the legend promised, and it had happened in her lifetime. But Marc hadn't seen the savage trail of destruction Arthur had left in the crowd of Dwyr Orr's followers at the harbor not so long ago. Her opinion of the ancient king had changed that day. She would never see him in the same way again.

"It is true," she replied, though flatly.

"Bah!" Medwyn said in disgust.

"I didn't see Arthur when Major Wright found him, but I did see pictures of him taken soon after he was rescued. And I saw him when he'd transformed to how he is now. It's the same person, and his recovery was miraculous."

"What about Merlin?" asked Marc. "Was he found at the same time?"

"No, Merlin arrived later."

How much should she tell him? Would it be useful or helpful for Marc and the others to know Merlin was an alien who had arrived from outer space? Medwyn wouldn't believe her anyway.

"It's a very, complicated long story," she said. "But there's no doubt in my mind they are who they say they are."

"If that's so," said Medwyn, "why are we going to all this effort? Why not leave everything to the old heroes?"

"Because we aren't babies lying in cradles," Meilyr replied, "sucking our thumbs while others do the hard work of freeing our country from its invaders."

"What are they doing now?" asked Marc. "Are they working to defeat the EAC? Will they be coming back?"

"I'm sorry, I don't know what they're doing. All I know is they were planning on returning to the Space Fleet."

"With the Dwyr in space too," said Madog, "maybe they'll try to attack her up there."

"Hmm, maybe." The conversation had reminded Taylan of Major Wright. She hoped he was okay and that Brigadier Colbourn was being less of a bitch than usual.

"Did you speak to Arthur or Merlin much?" Marc asked. "Did they tell you about the olden times?"

"Arthur did tell me some stories," she replied, "and he

talked about what life was like then. Merlin didn't really talk to anyone except Arthur, and when they spoke, they used the language of that time."

"Old Welsh?" Madog sounded interested. "Couldn't you understand it?"

"No, it sounded familiar, but I couldn't understand a word. It's nice to speak Welsh with all of you, though." She was growing uncomfortable with the conversation. She didn't like to think about Arthur. At the mention of his name, in her mind's eye she saw him sweeping through the crowd of Crusaders, a juggernaut of death and destruction, or she saw him leaning on his reddened sword at the foot of Dwyr Orr's platform, covered head to toe in blood and gore.

This was the reality of Arthur's time, she realized. Not the romantic tales of knights jousting at tournaments and rescuing fair maidens from tall towers. It had been a terrible time, a time of war, battles, and thousands of men dying in agony. And when the battles were over, peasants would search the bodies for things to steal. Then rats and crows would move in to feast on them.

She shivered and checked the position of the sun.

"Shouldn't we be leaving soon?" she suggested.

"Yes, you're right," said Meilyr. "Pack up, everyone."

"Maybe you could tell us some of Arthur's stories while we walk," Marc suggested to Taylan.

Meilyr answered for her. "No, we walk in silence, as quietly as we can. We're nearing the bridge, and that means plenty of Crusaders will be in the area, heading for Ynys Mon. If they hear the local language being spoken, they'll come straight for us."

Marc pulled a face, but he didn't protest.

Taylan knew how he felt. Some stories would have alleviated some of the boredom of the long night's walk. But Meilyr was right. The closer they got to Bryn Celli Ddu, the more careful they would need to be.

24

Kala opened the door to Perran's cabin. As she'd expected, she found her son asleep. After stepping softly to his bed, she gently shook him by the shoulder. When his eyes opened, she held a finger to her lips.

"Wh-what's going on?" he asked sleepily.

"We're going on a secret trip."

His large, dark eyes widened. "Where to? And why's it a secret?"

"It's more fun this way," she replied. "We're going home. I want you to pack only your most essential things, then we'll go to the shuttle bay. Hurry up."

She'd already packed what she needed for the journey to Earth. She guessed Morgan wouldn't discover that she and Perran had left the ship for several hours—she'd seen her take another member of the crew into her cabin only a few minutes ago—so now was her best chance for a long head start.

As she waited for Perran to gather the clothes and trinkets that were important to him, she wrinkled her nose at the memory of Morgan inviting the man in. How disgusting. There had been plenty of times she'd been tempted to do the same.

Leading the Crusade was a lonely occupation. But she had a position to uphold, standards to maintain. If she indulged herself, word would soon get out at the Dwyr didn't view what happened at the ceremonies to be a sacred act, that she was as base and ordinary as the next person. A single instance of indiscretion could mean the loss of her demigod-like status forever.

She had never explained Morgan's presence to her followers, but they had to perceive her as a close ally. As such, she should echo the Dwyr's behavior. Morgan was jeopardizing everything Kala had worked so hard for, just to satisfy her carnal needs.

"I'm ready," said Perran, carrying a bag as he walked toward her.

"Good boy."

"Are we going back to the last castle we were at?"

"Yes, the one where you made a friend. You'll be able to see her again. If she isn't awake when we arrive, I'll have her woken up and brought out to play with you."

Kala wasn't sure what time of day or night it would be when they reached West BI.

"Is Morgan coming too?" Perran asked as they left his cabin.

"Um, no. She's staying here. This trip's only for us."

"So she doesn't know the secret?"

"No, she doesn't."

Perran had been growing closer to Morgan over the weeks they'd spent aboard the *Belladonna*. Kala was certain their deepening relationship was entirely Morgan's doing. It was possible she only saw Perran as a substitute for her own son, who Arthur had murdered, but Kala suspected the woman had a bigger ambition in mind.

Her days as Dwyr were numbered if she didn't act. If she could just get to her books, she might learn how to defeat the interloper.

Perran looked troubled as they quickly walked the quiet passageways.

"Don't worry," said Kala. "Morgan won't mind that we're leaving. When she finds out we're gone, she'll think it's so funny, she'll laugh and laugh."

Perran didn't seem convinced. "Will we see her again?"

"Of course, darling. You don't need to worry about that."

Kala imagined Morgan back in a cave, thousands of meters below ground, trapped forever. Unable to die, she would probably go mad eventually.

The shuttle bay was open and empty. She'd only informed one of the pilots she wanted to return to Earth. She didn't know how far Morgan's tentacles extended through the crew. Recruiting people to spy on her and report her doings would be exactly the kind of thing the woman would do. She'd had to take a chance the pilot wasn't one of the spies.

She told Perran to climb the steps.

Once they were both inside, her racing heart began to slow. The pilot only had to complete the pre-flight checks, then they would be on their way.

Another big chance she was taking was that Morgan wouldn't arrive at the castle before her. It wouldn't take a genius to guess where she was going, and Morgan had the capability to travel through space without the need for a vessel to convey her.

That had been one of the capabilities Kala had thirsted deeply to learn. To know how to dissolve into a mist, to alter one's molecular structure while retaining the ability to move at will, and to survive the rigors of space! *That* would be something worth knowing. She would have loved to see the look on Ua Talman's face when she appeared at the *Bres,* alone with no shuttle. It would have wiped that condescending, self-satisfied smirk off his face.

But it was not to be.

She sighed.

"Ready to depart, ma'am?" came the pilot's voice over the intercom.

"Yes!" she called out. "I'm ready. Stop wasting time."

Irritably, she fastened her seat belt and told Perran to do the same.

The hatch closed, sealing them in. Just another few seconds, and they would be underway.

Kala waited impatiently for the engines to fire.

Silence.

What *was* the pilot doing? Didn't the man understand her haste? It was so hard to find reliable, intelligent staff.

"Would you please hurry up!" she shouted.

Nothing.

No, not nothing. She could hear movement in the pilot's cabin. It was the sound of something heavy being dragged over the floor.

Two figures appeared at the cabin door: the pilot, his head hanging at a crazy angle and his tongue protruding, and Morgan, her hand fastened around his neck. She had one arm outstretched, holding the man upright so his arms and legs hung loose, his knees bent as he was taller than her. *Had been* taller than her.

Kala couldn't move. She couldn't speak.

Perran calmly unfastened his seat belt, got up, and walked to Morgan's side.

"I'm sorry, Mother, but I don't want to leave without Morgan. She's fun, more fun than my friend on Earth."

"Thank you for telling me what your mother was doing," Morgan said to him. "You were right, it was a very silly joke. I don't think it's funny that you two would sneak away without me. In fact, I find it very rude."

She addressed her final comment to Kala, her tone turning harsh.

She turned to Perran. "Do you think it was rude?"

Perran nodded gravely, holding eye contact with Kala.

"What happens when people are rude?" Morgan asked.

"They have to be punished."

"That's what I was thinking. What a clever boy you are."

25

———

Crossing to Ynys Mon was going to be impossible without being seen. The tides in the Afon Menai were strong and fast, and even if they could have swum across at night, the water would damage the equipment they were carrying. They would have to go over the bridge. But so many Crusaders were arriving for the festival, there was never time it was empty.

Taylan and the brothers had watched the road for hours. Hordes of people were turning up. Meilyr had originally estimated a few thousand would celebrate midsummer at Bryn Celli Ddu. They'd been forced to revise that figure to tens of thousands.

The numbers increased their chances of being caught exponentially. On the other hand, if they were successful, the effects would be even more calamitous.

They waited until dark. That way, their clothes would not easily be seen. Though they resembled Crusaders physically, the cult members dressed differently. The Resistance fighters wore the industrially manufactured attire of the time before the invasion, while Crusaders seemed to prefer homespun, hand dyed textiles and handmade clothes.

How they planned on keeping up *that* habit while also eating all the sheep, Taylan had never figured out.

After debating whether to cross in a group or individually, they decided on the former. They were stronger as a unit, and it meant taking only one chance of being accosted. Marc was the best at faking a Crusader accent, so he would be the one to answer if anyone spoke to them.

When the road was fairly empty, they stepped out onto it from the hedgerow where they'd been hiding. Their packs would not look strange. Many Crusaders had hiked there and were also carrying packs. Keeping tight with their heads down to discourage attention, they set off.

The sky was clear and the moon was nearly full. Potholes dotted the road surface, and weeds sprouted in the cracks. As they walked, cars occasionally drove up behind them and they had to move aside. The vehicles would continue, swerving to avoid the holes. A group arrived on horseback, steadily clip clopping along. The Resistance fighters moved out of the way and watched the animals and their riders pass by.

They reached the bridge. It was only a couple of hundred meters long. They would soon be across it.

Taylan walked between the four men. Meilyr led the way, Medwyn and Magog walked to each side, and Marc brought up the rear. They couldn't risk her being recognized, even by the light of the moon.

The bridge stretched out in front of them. Ten or so people were already on it. The horseback riders were leaving the farther end. From behind came the sound of more travelers, chattering and laughing excitedly.

"Let's get this over with," murmured Meilyr.

To calm her nerves, Taylan focused on the Crusaders ahead. They straggled out in couples and one larger bunch, but they seemed to be together. Some were children, walking more slowly than their parents. She guessed they had to be tired after their long day's trek.

A sense of misgiving hit her.

When they reached Bryn Celli Ddu, they would plant incendiaries in the stands, displays, and storage facilities for the festival. When the people gathered to witness the sunrise, they would detonate the devices. The result would be chaos, panic, and plenty of injuries and deaths as the masses fought to escape the fires.

She knew how that felt. The scene of the pandemonium as Arthur had harvested lives as he passed through the crowd at the launch ceremony was indelibly etched on her mind. She'd nearly been killed in the crush herself, bodies piling on top of her. It had only been through luck she'd survived.

Her gaze was fixed on the Crusader kids walking ahead of her. They would be at the celebration too. Tired and not really understanding what was going on, probably not being able to see a thing, they would be there with their families when the fires broke out.

They wouldn't stand a chance.

Before she knew it, they were over the bridge.

"Phew," came Marc's soft exclamation from behind her.

Ditches edged the road on the Ynys Mon side, but at their farther banks were tall hedges. Meilyr checked behind and in front of him several times before slipping into a ditch and then climbing behind the cover of a hedge.

"We did it!" said Marc when they'd all followed him.

"Not yet," said Madog. "We still have a long night ahead of us."

"Let's rest a while and check everything over," said Meilyr.

As they squatted down and began to pull the incendiaries out of their packs, Medwyn said, "We mustn't forget to steal some supplies for the return journey before we set these things off."

"Good point," Madog agreed. "I don't fancy eating burnt biscuits all the way back!"

"I..." Taylan paused "...I'm having second thoughts. I'm not sure this is such a good idea."

The men stopped what they were doing.

"Well, in that case," said Medwyn, "let's pack up and go home. The great Taylan Ellis has spoken, fellas."

"What's wrong?" Meilyr asked.

"Yeah, what's your problem?" Medwyn demanded.

Meilyr told him to shut up.

"There are kids here," Taylan replied.

"Crusader kids," said Medwyn.

"What did you expect?" asked Madog. "It's a festival. People bring their children to festivals."

Meilyr was regarding her gravely.

"I don't know," Taylan said. "I don't know what I expected. I suppose I didn't really think it through."

Medwyn said, "That sounds like your pr—"

"I said shut up," Meilyr spat. "Taylan, do you think Dwyr Orr cared about what happened to our kids when she invaded? I'm surprised you, of all people, would balk at endangering Crusader children. For all you know, your own could be—"

"Don't say it," Taylan interrupted. "I know what you mean. Maybe there's no point in me searching for them because they've gone somewhere they can never be found. But I think it's *because* of my children—"

"You're not the only parent here," said Madog. "I had three kids. A boy and two girls. All shot dead before my eyes."

"God, I'm sorry. I didn't know."

Madog thrust the incendiary he was holding into his pack before walking away into the field.

Taylan silently cursed.

Then a realization hit her. Was *that* why she hadn't been able to find her children?

"What if my kids were taken in by a Crusader couple? What if they're hiding them from the Dwyr and that's why she hasn't found them yet?"

"Then they wouldn't bring them here, would they?" said Medwyn, his jaw clenched.

"I don't know. They're just kids. Who would take any notice of them? And they will have grown and changed since... Maybe it would look strange if the couple didn't attend the festival, so they took a chance and brought them along."

"Now you're scraping the barrel," said Medwyn.

Throughout the discussion, Marc had remained silent with his head bowed.

He looked up. "Taylan's right. We shouldn't hurt children. It's wrong."

"Oh, for..." Medwyn turned to Meilyr. "Don't tell me you're listening to this rubbish. We came here to do a job. Are we doing it or not?"

Meilyr didn't answer.

"Forget I asked. *I* came here to do a job, and I'm doing it. And so's Madog. The rest of you can go to hell."

26

———

"You told us it wouldn't be like this," Charles thundered. "You told us they would listen."

Hans was resting his forehead on his palms. It was a disaster, but none of it was his fault. He'd done his best in the circumstances. What could he have done differently? He retraced each step since Mariya had taken him to the cave in the mountains and the Jamaicans had locked him in a cage.

Each choice he'd made had either been out of necessity or for the long-term good of everyone. No other option had been open to him except to remain with the Resistance. He could never have survived alone. The EAC would have picked him up and tortured him in no time. He'd been forced to pay lip service to the fighters' dreams of independence for Jamaica. They would never have accepted him otherwise. And if he'd crossed to the Alliance's side when they arrived, he would have been lynched.

It was a mess.

"Hans," said Devon gravely, "what should we do? We can't go on much longer like this."

He looked out across the landscape to far-off Kingston as he considered his answer.

Charles and Devon had come to speak to him at his villa. He'd returned there after the fighting had finished and made the place his home again. The place had been entirely ransacked. All his luxurious furniture and fittings had been stolen or vandalized, the anger and resentment of Jamaica's underclass taken out on them with a vengeance.

After burning the worst-damaged items, he'd been left with some things to sit, sleep, and eat on, and that was all he really needed. He'd looked forward to slowly refurbishing the house over time, as the situation on the island improved. He'd even dreamed of spending evenings on the veranda, a gin and tonic in hand, gazing out on the country he'd helped to rebuild. It would have been a happy, prosperous nation, part of the great republic of the Britannic Alliance.

He would have wished Mariya was there with him to see it, and that would have been the only blemish on the perfect scene.

"*Hans,*" said Devon.

"I haven't decided yet. I need more time to think about it."

"We don't have time," Charles insisted. "People are dying. We need the Alliance's doctors and pharmaceuticals. Three-quarters of the island still has no power. The farmers are too scared to go out in their fields until they're checked for ordnance. If they don't sow crops soon, in a few months we'll have a massive famine. We need clean water. We need help! Why won't the BA help us?"

Devon's jaw muscle worked as he sat next to Hans, cracking his knuckles. "We pushed too hard," he muttered. "We said too much too soon."

He was right. He'd hit the nail on the head. The Alliance's attitude toward its territories and protectorates was paternalistic. It would not stand for its dependents getting 'uppity', and its feelings would take a long time to change. Hans could have brought about that change, over years, perhaps decades. But the opportunity had been denied him.

If only the Royal Marines' major had delivered his message. The ministers and military chiefs would have known he was playing a game, stringing the Jamaicans along, that he was working to bring them into the fold. Those men and women of the BA Government were used to subterfuge and artifice. They would have understood, nodded and smiled, knowing what it all meant. They would have agreed to support Jamaica.

Everything had hung on that message.

"Barbados caved yesterday," Charles announced.

"They did?" asked Devon. "I didn't know."

"Yes, they accepted the BA's terms. What choice did they have? They're worse off than we are."

"The Bahamas will be next," said Devon.

Charles didn't reply, his features cloudy.

Then he blurted, "We'll be last in line, begging for scraps. And it's down to him!" He jabbed a finger at Hans.

"Charles," Devon demurred, "Hans has always tried to help us."

"No, he hasn't. He's always tried to help himself. He was the one speaking out at the meeting. He was the one—"

"He was standing up for Jamaicans. Mariya believed in him."

"Yes. And look where that got her."

"You can't blame him for her death. She was killed by a Crusader, and the raid on the EAC headquarters wasn't even his idea."

Hans was touched by Devon's loyalty. Touched—and ashamed. Though it was hard to admit to himself, he knew he didn't deserve it. He'd always been self-serving, thinking only of himself and his grand plan for the Alliance, prepared to sacrifice everyone else to his schemes. Mariya had known it. She'd been smart. She'd seen through him, but she'd allowed him to pretend he was devoted to Jamaica because he could be useful.

He put a hand on Devon's shoulder. "Thank you for sticking up for me. I appreciate it, my friend."

Charles scowled.

Hans rose to his feet. "I agree we're at somewhat of an impasse with the Alliance. Extricating ourselves without conceding too much will take some delicate negotiating, which requires careful planning. I don't want to be rude, but I need some time alone. Time to gather my thoughts and figure out the best way to proceed."

"Hmpf," said Charles. "His Lordship is dismissing us. Let's go, Devon."

As Devon drained his drink, Charles went on, "We'll be back in the morning to hear your ideas about what we do next. They'd better be good ones, and they'd better get us a fast solution to the crisis."

Or what? Hans wondered.

The two Jamaicans descended the wooden steps.

"See you tomorrow, Hans," said Devon.

"See you then, Devon, Charles."

The latter didn't reply. A few moments later, Mariya's car pulled out of the driveway onto the mountain road.

Hans went inside the villa. Surveying the expansive space, now sparsely filled with the detritus of his former life as Head of SIS, he took stock. His possessions had been whittled down to almost nothing.

What would he need?

He walked to his bedroom. At the bottom of one of the wardrobes was a large, canvas bag. He took it out, opened it on his bed, and began to pack. When he'd filled the base with the few clothes he owned, he placed an interface on top of them.

He went to the kitchen. There, he gathered packets of dry food, snacks, candy bars, and two large, plastic bottles of water.

After a brief hesitation, he also picked up a knife. Returning to his bedroom, he put the knife and all the provisions in his bag.

From his bathroom, he took a bag of toiletries and a comb.

He returned to the veranda. His driveway remained empty. No cars were passing on the road. The mountainside was quiet. No one was about.

Going into the bathroom once more, he lowered the lid on the toilet and climbed onto it. He pushed up a ceiling tile, and groped blindly in the space above. His fingers brushed cloth. Grasping it, he dragged a large pouch closer. It was heavy and resisted his pull. When it reached the hole, he lifted it down carefully.

He sat on the toilet lid, loosened the pouch's strings, and examined its contents. Gold, platinum, and jewels glinted at him. It was a fortune, enough to buy several villas.

Hans had never considered himself materialistic, but that didn't mean he hadn't learned from the experiences of his immigrant ancestors. The wisdom to always keep a portion of your wealth portable, in case of emergencies, had been passed down through the generations. His family had never belonged to the privileged elite, they'd never enjoyed the sense of certainty about the future that came from being a member of the inner circle, but in this case, it had saved him.

He tied the strings of the pouch and tucked it into a corner of his bag.

What else?

He only needed three more things. He crossed his bedroom to a set of drawers. From the top drawer, he took a photograph, a silver necklace, and a small ceramic pot.

"You're coming with me, my dear," he murmured.

He was ready to leave.

27

———

Lorcan seethed as he sat in his shuttle, taking the long trip to Earth. Iolani had insisted on coming with him to the Kamboto Mine. She'd threatened to abandon the Project, taking Camilla and Anders with her, and tell the media all about her kidnapping if he refused to allow her to come along.

You can hardly expect me to trust you after everything you've done, she'd said.

He would have to go to the mine and sort out the child labor problem with her in tow, scrutinizing his every move. Worse, with her accompanying him, he couldn't in good conscience take any security or support people with him. The association with what he'd done to her would be too great. So it would be just the two of them.

He rued the day he'd set foot inside her house in Suriname, eager to meet the great Iolani Hale. She and her damned dogs had become the bane of his existence. If only he could turn back time. Given the chance, he would choose to never go to see her, or at least leave her alone in her jungle hermitage.

But then he might never have discovered the flaws in the

Project. He had to concede his experiences with Hale might have prevented a catastrophic disaster and tragedy.

Possibly.

It was certainly better to be safe than sorry.

And then, there was Camilla Lebedev. Without Hale's interference, he would never have come to know her.

The only positive side to making the journey to the surface with Hale was that Camilla had decided to accompany them. She would spend a few days visiting family and friends, and then she would return with them to the *Bres* when they'd finished their business at the mine.

"I remember the last time I was aboard this shuttle," Hale remarked to her friend, seated next to her across the aisle from Lorcan. "I think it was this one, wasn't it?" she asked him.

He gritted his teeth and didn't answer.

"It was an uncomfortable ride," Hale remarked.

"Was it?" asked Camilla. "These seats are pretty comfy. It certainly makes a nice change from flying economy. That's all funding institutions will ever pay for when I attend conferences. Cattle class travel and budget hotels."

"Oh yeah," said Hale. "Last time I was here, I felt quite *constricted*."

"I'd hate to subject you to another uncomfortable voyage," said Lorcan. "If you like, I can ask the pilot to take us back to the ship and you can disembark."

"No, it's fine. I don't know why, but this time around I feel much more free."

"Great," Lorcan said between his teeth. "Why not get up and walk around a bit?" *Right outside the airlock would be perfect.*

Perhaps noticing his tenseness, Camilla said, "I'm sure you'll both sort out the mix-up at the mine quickly. It's probably just a misunderstanding."

"Huh!" said Iolani, sounding utterly unconvinced.

"I'm confident it's exactly that," Lorcan said. "The AP's

hiring policies are very clear. I'm surprised they're using human labor at all. Technology exists that can perform almost all tasks that used to be undertaken by miners."

"They're using children because it's cheaper," said Iolani, as if it were the most obvious explanation in the world.

"Cheaper than machines?" asked Lorcan. "I don't think so."

Hale rolled her eyes. "You don't have a clue, do you?"

Camilla coughed. "I'll be glad to set foot on Terra firma again."

Lorcan pulled out ear buds from the receptacle in his arm rest and pushed them into his ears.

USUALLY, when Lorcan visited any of the many and various Project subsidiary companies, he would inform the relevant manager of his plans. This wasn't out of consideration for the person, but simply because his time was precious. He didn't want to waste it waiting around for the relevant person to be called in to speak to him or to provide access to secure areas. He had inspectors to check everything was running smoothly and conforming to the locality's laws and regulations.

This time, he would give no notice. Regardless of what he discovered, he would fire the team responsible for inspecting the Kamboto Mine. There was no question about that. But he'd held off on making any staffing changes because he didn't want the manager to suspect something was up. He wanted to see the mine operating exactly as it did every day, when Ua Talman was not present to witness its transgressions.

He'd hired a four-wheel drive at the airport nearest the mine. A tiny place with a landing strip only long enough for light aircraft and no pad for a space shuttle, it was nevertheless more than a hundred kilometers from their destination. With nothing more than small, poor villages en route, they would be forced to sleep in the car. The prospect did nothing to improve Lorcan's feelings about Hale's presence on the trip.

She sat next to him in stoic silence as tens of kilometers of road passed beneath the car's wheels.

At first, he maintained the same attitude. He had no desire to even make small talk with her—he hated small talk at the best of times—let alone discuss anything important, like her work on the *Bres* or, heaven forbid, the unpleasant interactions they'd had.

But, eventually, he couldn't stand the monotony of nothing but the endless crunch of tires on dirt road any longer. Also, there was something about simply sitting next to her, neither of them speaking, that drove a spike into his conscience.

"Iolani, I know this will probably sound hollow, but I honestly had no idea that children were being employed at the Kamboto Mine. All the Project's subsidiaries have strict protocols to follow and standards to meet. If they fail in those regards, they're dropped. I don't know what went wrong at Kamboto, but I hope to find out. As a minimum, the mine will cease operation from the time of our arrival and will not start up again until these problems are rectified."

Some of the stiffness in her figure seemed to ease. She replied, "I appreciate it's difficult for you to admit failure, but it isn't me you should be telling all this to, it's those children and their families."

"No, it's important you hear it too. As to the people affected, in the case of any deaths or injuries, they will be fully compensated…"

She tutted and shook her head. "That's what it always comes down to with you, isn't it? Money. You think money will solve everything."

"It doesn't solve everything, but it goes a long way to helping. What would you have me do? I can't change what's happened."

"You can change what will happen, though. Look around, Lorcan. This is a poor country, full of poor people and a handful of very rich people who exploit everyone else. That's why you ended up employing children. Do you think their parents don't love them, and that's why they allowed them to go down into a pit?"

"I'm not responsible for the decisions of their parents. I can say with absolute certainty I would never have allowed—" He choked as long-buried emotions rushed to the surface.

Hale glanced at him. She waited as he got himself under control.

"These problems are complicated," she conceded, "but unless people like you take them on, they'll never be solved. Ripping precious resources out of the earth and permanently removing them from the planet by using what amounts to slave labor, isn't the answer."

"That's quite the burden you'd like to place on my shoulders," said Lorcan. "The welfare of all humanity."

"You're fond of saying the Project is humanity's destiny. You're happy enough to be responsible for *that*. The well being of others is a burden we should *all* shoulder, morally. If we aren't prepared to help our fellow human beings, what's the point? That's what we're about, isn't it? That's what civilization is—people helping each other."

"Civilization is about progress, improving the lot of your own people, your tribe, often to the detriment of others. That's the natural order of things in human behavior. The Project is the inevitable result of billions of years of evolution."

Again, she shook her head. "If you think that, you don't understand evolution. Human intelligence is not some pinnacle of achievement evolution trends toward. It's only a chance outcome of natural selection. The time humans have existed is a mere blip in the history of life on Earth. Other species have been and continue to be far more successful than us in evolutionary terms. The jury is still out on whether intelligence alone is a marker for survival over the long term. Several times in the last few thousand years, we've come close to throwing ourselves back into the stone ages. For instance, look at what *you're* doing."

His hands tightened into fists.

Here we go again.

"As well as depleting the planet of finite resources, the Project is destroying the environment wherever it operates. And for what? So you can build your ships, which, without intervention, would probably have become humankind's largest cemeteries. If you want to argue that human evolution is moving in a particular direction, all the signs indicate it's headed for self-annihilation. An evolutionary dead end."

Silence fell again. Lorcan just didn't know what to say in reply.

After a couple of minutes, Iolani added, "You're in a unique position. You're one of the very few people who can make a real difference. You have the power and authority to reverse the tide. Whether you decide to try, well, that's up to you."

28

———

With little hope of catching up to Taylan before she was on her way back to the Preseli Hills, Wright had decided to try to meet her as she returned. It would have made more sense to wait at the Resistance hideout, as the chances of finding someone who was trying to keep out of sight in the wilderness were small. But Merlin was confident they could do it.

The plan was, if she agreed to come with them to the *Gallant* and take part in the third attempt to assassinate the Dwyr, they would cut across country to the coast and then work their way down to the rendezvous point for their passage back to Ireland.

If she agreed to come with them.

Wright wasn't certain he wanted to try to persuade her. His sense of conviction about the mission was half-hearted at best.

On their second day of travel, heading north across the rocky, rolling landscape, Arthur acted as he had when they'd drawn close to the Resistance hideout. He halted, his broad back straightening and his eyes narrowing as he surveyed their surroundings. He spoke to Merlin, using his first language.

Wright hated it when they did that. He felt excluded, though he didn't think it was deliberate, only that Arthur was more comfortable using his mother tongue.

After a few sentences, back and forth, Arthur said to Wright, "I would like to make a small detour. I don't think it will take us much out of our way."

"It may be beneficial in helping us find Taylan," said Merlin. "Arthur is better than I at reading the land."

"Fine by me," Wright replied, feeling he was increasingly losing control of the situation. But he didn't know how to regain a hold on things. Arthur and Merlin were not Marines. They were like unstoppable forces, and he had no idea where they were leading him, the Alliance, or the planet.

THE DETOUR WAS NOT AS short as Arthur had predicted. They'd halted as the sun rose high, stayed hidden during most of the day, and traveled an hour into dusk before they found the place.

The huge trees loomed dark in the fading light. They'd spotted them from higher ground a kilometer away. There were ten or twelve, standing in a circle. As they drew closer, their age became evident. The original trunks had died and hollowed, and side trunks had taken over the trees' growth.

Could they really have existed during Arthur's time? Wright didn't know if trees could live so long, but he guessed they could, or perhaps new trees had grown or been planted in the same place.

They stepped through a gap between the massive branches, thick with dark green, needle-like leaves. In the center was a clearing, and in the middle of the clearing stood stone ruins, no higher than Wright's waist. They reminded him of the little church in the Preseli Hills where Merlin had retrieved Arthur's sword and armor from their hiding place.

"Looks like this is it," he said. "What do we do now?"

"I'd like to stay here tonight," said Arthur.

"That's it?" Wright asked. He'd been expecting the king or Merlin to say there was something else to find that had been hidden for thousands of years.

"That's all," said Arthur. "Just one night."

He took some wire from his pack—he'd asked the Resistance fighters for it—before disappearing for a while as Wright and Merlin set up camp under one of the trees. The ground was tinder dry, the branches and foliage so dense, no rain ever penetrated.

After they'd eaten, Arthur got up and walked away again with no explanation of where he would be going or when he planned on coming back. The night was cloudy and the area beyond their camp looked pitch black. It was impossible to see where Arthur had gone.

"What's this about?" Wright asked Merlin quietly. "Why are we here?"

"That's for Arthur to tell you, if he wishes."

"So you know?"

"He hasn't told me, but I can guess."

Wright made a guess of his own. "Are those ruins we saw the remains of a church?"

"Yes, I believe so, though I don't recall ever coming here."

"So he's praying again?"

"Perhaps. I'm afraid I really don't know for sure, Major."

The last time Arthur had prayed, he'd gone on to slaughter scores of people. That was what Taylan had said, anyway. Maybe the king was anticipating they would encounter a lot of Crusaders soon. Or maybe not. Merlin seemed to think it was something different this time.

Wright had been thinking about what the alien had

revealed to him a few days ago, about powers he represented that wanted the Alliance to succeed. He'd been reminded of something else that Taylan had told him.

"You aren't the only extra-terrestrial life form here on Earth, are you?" he asked Merlin.

"Did I say I was?" the alien lay down on his side, propping himself up on one elbow. "Do you humans really think you're alone in the galaxy?"

Wright ignored his baiting. "At Dwyr Orr's invasion launch ceremony, Ellis said she saw a woman with the Dwyr who, when everything went to shit, dissolved into a mist and floated away. That sounds like what you can do. Ellis said the EAC have an alien on their side too. Is that right?"

"Ah yes. Unfortunately, that is so."

Surprised by the unusual candor, Wright pressed on, "Does this being represent a power that opposes your own? Are the two of you in some kind of fight for control of Earth?"

"That's a simplistic interpretation. I prefer to see the situation more philosophically. But your species grasps things better when they're stated in black and white terms, so let's allow that to stand."

"I'm no genius, but even I understand there are shades of gray in most things. I don't think we're as dumb as you seem to think we are."

"And yet, here you are, murdering each other in cold blood every second of every day. Perhaps your appreciation of the level of humanity's development is, shall we say, more hopeful than realistic?"

Wright wanted nothing more than to wipe the smirk off Merlin's face, but he couldn't deny the truth of what he was saying. However, he wasn't about to allow the alien to get away with his insults scot-free.

"You don't seem to have much of a problem with helping

Arthur to kill when it suits you. What is it you do to him that protects him from pulse fire?"

The alien turned onto his back. "Impossible to explain, sorry."

Yet he didn't deny he was doing *something*.

Merlin closed his eyes. He wasn't about to go to sleep. He didn't sleep. He didn't appear to have any need for it. And neither did he ever eat or drink anything that Wright saw.

Guessing he wasn't about to get any more information from the creature, Wright got into his sleeping bag. As a mere human, *he* needed sleep.

Something moving in the night woke him up. He opened his eyes and tried to figure out what it was. He could hear soft rustling nearby. Probably a fox searching for a snack. Peering into the darkness didn't reveal anything suspicious.

He turned onto his side, preparing to get a few more hours of rest while Arthur did his thing, when unprompted, Hans Jonte popped into his mind.

The message!

He'd forgotten to pass on Jonte's message to Colbourn.

Shit.

After everything that had happened in Jamaica, he'd been in a bad state by the time he made it back to the *Gallant*. The message had entirely slipped his mind. Was it a bad screw-up? It was hard to tell. Jonte had made sure to remind him before he left the field hospital, so he guessed it was important to the ex-head of SIS that word got through to the Alliance that he continued to work on their behalf.

But surely the man had encountered other BA military personnel. He'd probably told them the same thing and his message had been passed on.

Whatever the gravity of the mistake, there was nothing Wright could do about it now. He couldn't risk comming

Colbourn from West BI. A single signal to the *Gallant* would be easy to identify and track for the origin location.

He closed his eyes and tried to get more sleep.

When he woke a few hours later, Merlin was gone but Arthur had returned. Pre-dawn light filtered through the canopy. Arthur was awake, his hands behind his head, deep in thought.

"Did you do what you came here to do?" Wright asked.

"Yes, in a sense, though what I need to do cannot be done. Rather, what I did cannot be undone. But I feel better for coming here."

At Wright's puzzled silence, he said, "I'm speaking in riddles, aren't I? I'm sorry, my friend. Have you ever done anything you deeply regretted?"

Wright thought of the campaign to retake Jamaica. He thought of Patel falling backward into his arms, her face gone. He thought of his last sight of Elphicke, climbing down through the open manhole. At one point, he would have been able to justify to himself what he'd done. Now, he was finding it hard.

He replied, "Too many things."

"It's a part of being human," said Arthur.

"That's what Merlin would say."

"It's part of trying to do right. But what I did here was not because I wanted to do right. I committed a great sin, my unnatural son was born, and the result was the loss of everything I had worked for. My kingdom fell."

Wright could take a stab at what the 'sin' was, but he didn't understand what the rest of it meant. He guessed Taylan probably knew. If they ever found her, he might ask her, but he didn't want to probe too deeply into what seemed to be a sensitive subject.

"If you're ready to move on," he said, "we should do that.

We can get two or three hours of walking in before broad daylight. I wonder where Merlin's got to?"

"I'll look for him," said Arthur.

While he was gone, Wright broke camp.

He'd been waiting for his companions to return for a while when Arthur came back alone. Or, not entirely alone. He was carrying three dead rabbits. He smiled with boyish glee.

"The wire you have these days works better than the twine we used to use in my time." He removed the wire from the animals' necks and gutted them before tying them by their back feet to his belt. "We can eat them later."

"No sign of Merlin?"

"No, I couldn't—"

The alien poked his head under an overhanging branch. "All ready?"

29

———

"I told you once, *I* am mistress here," said Morgan softly. "I hope from now on, you will remember that."

Kala glared at her, but she swallowed the response that came naturally to her lips, instead forcing out, "I will remember."

Her time in the *Belladonna's* brig had taught her a lot. It had taught her that what she'd feared the most, that Morgan would get Perran under her control, had already happened. At some time in their weeks aboard the ship, in the course of teaching her son telepathy, his affection had transferred to her usurper.

She had also learned that Morgan found it easy to make those around her do her bidding. Kala's crew had carried her, fighting and struggling, to a cell and locked her away. The people she'd thought slavishly adored her had been turned against her in an instant.

The final thing she'd come to understand during her time of incarceration was that she was nowhere near ready to give up. She would rather die than allow Morgan to steal her child and her domain from her.

"Do you agree to never attempt to leave this ship without my permission?" asked Morgan.

"I do."

"That you will never spend time with your son unless I am present?"

Kala's chest constricted. "I agree."

"That you will do exactly as I say regarding the running of the Crusade?"

"I will."

"Then you may be released," said Morgan.

The guard unlocked the door.

For a week, Kala had sat behind the transparent wall, on view to all who passed by, humiliated as a display to men and women who had once worshipped her.

She stepped through the gap.

"What's that on your arms?" Morgan asked.

Kala pulled her sleeves down, but Morgan pushed her right sleeve up again.

Off and on, for days, Kala had scratched her arms and legs, taking out her anger and frustration on her body. She'd dug her fingernails into her skin, clawing at her flesh, only achieving satisfaction when her blood ran freely.

"Why have you done this?" asked Morgan, pushing up Kala's left sleeve. She held Kala's gaze questioningly.

"Weren't you the one who said the Crusade needed a blood sacrifice?"

"This is not sacrifice. This is something else."

Morgan passed a hand over the damaged skin. Kala felt a tingling sensation as it healed and became whole again. She was angry. The wounds *meant* something to her, something she couldn't put into words. She didn't want Morgan to control her body as well as her behavior. She didn't tell her she'd also hurt her legs.

"Do not do that again," said Morgan.

"Where's Perran?"

"He's in my cabin, practicing something I taught him earlier today."

Kala stiffened.

"You may return to your suite," Morgan said as they left the brig. "I want you to take the rest of the day to reflect on what's happened. It's a shame things had to come to this. I thought I'd made it clear when you released me how things were going to be, but obviously I didn't make it clear enough. We *can* get along, providing you adopt the right attitude. I'm not interested in leading the Crusade. I have no desire to be worshipped. Your people's love means nothing to me, and your ceremonies are boring. But I will not be deceived, and I will not be pushed aside. In truth, your behavior saddens me. You are my kin, though far distant. We should be allies, not enemies."

"I...would like to be your ally," Kala said.

Morgan gave her a look that implied she didn't quite believe her.

Could Morgan read her mind?

Kala hoped not. She had the impression from her sessions on telepathy that it couldn't happen without both subjects being willing.

"It would definitely be preferable if we could get along," Morgan said. "We have much work to do if the Crusade is to achieve its goals."

Kala was hanging to a shred of hope. She judged that Morgan considered Perran too young to assume the role she had in mind for him; that she still needed Kala for the time being. When her usefulness ran out, that would be the end of her. She had until then to get rid of Morgan, but from now on she would have to tread exceptionally carefully.

They'd reached her suite.

"Relax," Morgan said. "Think. I know you'll see the wisdom of our new way forward."

As soon as she'd gone, Kala sat on the edge of her bed, gripping the silken coverlet tightly. She waited several minutes, thinking things over. When she thought Morgan had to be out of hearing distance, she requested refreshments.

The man who brought them to her looked a little familiar, but she hadn't paid much attention to the lower ranks aboard her flagship. They had been of no importance to her, until now.

"What's your name?" she asked, as the man put down the tray on her bedside table.

Without meeting her gaze, he replied, "Cookson, ma'am."

"Cookson, do you know where I've been for the past week?"

"I do, ma'am."

"And what do you think about that?"

"I think it's a terrible shame. I...we all do, but no one was able to stop it."

"No one was able to stop it? Explain."

"We can't seem to do what we want to do whenever that woman, Morgan, has anything to do with it."

"I see. So, you wanted to release me from the brig, but you found you couldn't?"

"Something like that. It was more like, we would go there, and then we would forget why we were there, until we left again. Then we would remember, and return, only for the same thing to happen. It's strange."

The man's words brought her joy. So Morgan hadn't managed to turn her followers against her. She was only exerting some sort of mind control over them. If that was the case, there had to be a limit to what she could do, either by distance, or number of people she could influence, or to what extent. At some point, they would return to Earth, and then, possibly, Kala could harness the support of the Crusaders against her latest enemy. And if she could find out who had imprisoned Morgan all those years ago, all the better.

There was hope yet.

"Thank you. You're dismissed," she told Cookson.

The biggest problem was Perran. Kala doubted Morgan was controlling her son's mind. The bond she'd created with him meant she didn't need to. The boy was young and easily impressed. He thirsted for the knowledge Morgan could teach, in the same way she had herself. The enticement held great sway over him and Morgan had been quick to exploit it.

Kala could destroy Morgan and regain control of her life, but it would mean nothing if she lost Perran.

30

———

Bryn Celli Ddu didn't look like much, in Taylan's opinion. From the outside, it was just a long, grassy mound. She guessed the inside had to be more impressive. She'd heard the standing stone the sun would light up when it rose tomorrow was carved in incredibly ancient symbols, predating even Arthur's time. But her chances of getting a look at it were zero. Thousands of Crusaders thronged the site, barely held back by the ropes and guards that ringed the mound.

Brightly colored pavilions dotted the fields all around, housing stalls selling food, drink, trinkets, souvenirs, textiles, and camping supplies. Some of the pavilions were for entertainment purposes. Strains of music and the laughter of audiences watching performances could be heard coming from them. Others seemed to have nefarious purposes, judging from the closed entrances, the hawkers standing outside, and the glances to the left and right of any customers who ventured in.

The low rise Taylan was standing on was around half a kilometer from the festival site, but scents from it still reached her: barbecuing meat, wood smoke, incense.

What struck her most forcibly was how *old* it all looked. There was very little technology on show, perhaps only the security guards' pulse rifles. No screens or holos, no electronic toys for the kids, nothing that required electricity to run. The cars some of the attendees had arrived in had been parked far away, out of sight. It was like watching a history docuvid based on pre-industrial times.

Beyond the pavilions, a sea of tents stretched to the horizon with figures moving between them.

She had a brief vision of flames leaping from tent to tent and people running, screaming, on fire.

"I'm sorry, I just can't do it."

Meilyr stood next to her.

"I understand."

He'd asked her to think over her decision and, out of respect for him, she had. She felt churlish. She'd asked to come along and take part in this attack on the Crusaders. Her inclusion could have placed an additional burden on the brothers, though, as it turned out, she didn't think that had been the case in the end.

"I'll help steal supplies for the trek back to the hideout," she said.

"You don't have a problem with that too?" asked Meilyr, seeming to want to make light of the situation.

"I don't have a problem with stealing and I don't have a problem with attacking the other side's military, but this? Look. There are little kids here. Babies. And these people...most of them have probably never held a weapon. They've moved in from Europe after the invasion. I don't know why they follow the Dwyr. They're probably just deluded. People can be incredibly dumb. That doesn't mean they deserve to die."

"Let me ask you something," said Meilyr. "If you or I were to walk among those Crusaders now and tell them who we are, what do you think they would do?"

Taylan swallowed. He had a point. She recalled standing on the quayside at Dwyr Orr's invasion launch, waiting for the right moment to shoot the woman, knowing the crowd would rip her limb from limb if they knew her intention.

"What would they do, Taylan?" he pressed.

"They would kill us. I can't deny it, but that's because—"

"Because they're deluded? Or because, deep down, they're depraved and vicious?"

"Maybe their beliefs have made them like that. But people can change. If they could be taught a different understanding of the world, they would change."

"I think you give them too much credit," said Meilyr. "The older ones didn't grow up like that. They saw and heard what Dwyr Orr's way had to offer, and they chose it of their own free will. They weren't indoctrinated. Her methods appealed to them. All the invasions, murdering and enslaving the local populaces, turning back the wheel of progress. They *want* all that. And you know that if our positions were reversed and Crusaders were standing here watching a crowd of *our* people preparing for a celebration, they would not be having this discussion. They would not hesitate to hurt us."

The memory of the search patrol who had hunted her down flashed into her mind, their joy at wounding her and cold debate over whether to kill her. They'd seen her as less than human, an *other*.

"I know," she conceded. "I know you're right. But that doesn't mean we have to be the same as them. We can be better. If we stoop to their level, we've become like them. Then they've won, haven't they?"

"As I see it, if we *don't* stoop to their level, they will win."

"You sound like Medwyn," she said bitterly. She'd thought Meilyr was better than this.

"I see his point of view, but I don't believe we're the same. Medwyn won't feel a thing for any Crusaders who die tomorrow, but I will feel sad for the innocent lives lost. I'm not completely callous. However, death is inevitable in war, and we didn't start this war, though I hope we'll finish it."

He stepped down from the rise and left.

Taylan's heart sank. She hated going against the brothers. Most of them had been nothing but kind to her. If it hadn't been for Marc finding her after she'd been shot and Meilyr nursing her back to health, she'd be dead. She'd been hoping Meilyr might change his mind when he heard her thoughts, but he'd come down on Medwyn's side. Madog couldn't be blamed for feeling the same.

The sun disappeared behind a cloud and a chill wind started up.

Thoughts of the people who would die in the morning already grieved her, and she hadn't forgotten her earlier fear that, by some remote chance, her own children might be among the throng.

It wasn't only a matter of refusing to take part in the scheme, she couldn't allow it to happen. She had to stop Meilyr and the others from planting the devices tonight. But how could she do that? She'd tried reasoning with them and it hadn't worked, except perhaps for Marc. He seemed to agree with her. She couldn't physically stop the men. It would be three against one. Could she hide or destroy the devices? It was unlikely. Medwyn would keep a close eye on them now he knew her feelings.

She traced Meilyr's steps, leaving the high ground.

In a few hours, most of the Crusaders would be sleeping. They would go to bed early in readiness for the midsummer sunrise. The brothers would sneak into the areas closest to the mounds and hide the incendiaries. When the celebration was at its height they would set them off by remote control, and terror and bedlam would ensue.

She couldn't allow it to happen.

Returning to the hidden place near the hedgerow where the brothers were waiting for the right time to make their move, Taylan's stomach churned with discomfort.

What the hell was she doing?

She was trying to figure out a way to protect Crusaders, the very people who had killed her friends and neighbors and separated her from her children. They supported Dwyr Orr, who had tortured Wilson horribly and committed who knew how many more atrocities.

Her feelings were all screwed up. She wished she could talk to Abacha, but he was far away aboard the *Valiant* while the ship underwent repairs. Even to cuddle Boots might help, but she didn't know where the cat was anymore.

She was alone, and she had to decide the right thing to do, and then how to do it.

31

―――――

"What I don't understand is," said Wright, "why we're trying to kill the Dwyr but not this other alien who's with her."

Merlin and Arthur were walking ahead of him along a trail between two high hills. Arthur's long stride and Merlin's apparently inexhaustible stamina meant he was often lagging behind them. It was hard to keep in top shape when you spent most of your time living on a starship, and they'd already walked over a hundred kilometers. Still, tomorrow was midsummer's day, and Taylan would begin her return journey soon. They probably only had another few days' walk ahead of them until their paths crossed hers...somehow.

"I said," Wright remarked, preparing to repeat himself—

"I heard you," Merlin replied without looking back. "But I don't quite understand. Why would we try to kill the Dwyr's companion?"

"Because she has to be mixed up in all this too. She was at the launch ceremony, Ellis said. Right beside the Dwyr. Who knows, she might even be responsible for the Dwyr's messed-up thinking."

"In my experience, humans are quite capable of messed-up thinking all by themselves."

Choosing to ignore the insult, Wright went on, "How do we know this alien isn't the power behind the throne, so to speak?"

That certainly seemed to be how things were with Merlin and Arthur. It was their relationship that had prompted his line of thought. Arthur did whatever Merlin told him to do, basically.

"Maybe we've been targeting the wrong person all along," he said. He hadn't forgotten Merlin's refusal to enter the Dwyr's castle grounds, saying there was a barrier he couldn't cross. What had that been about? Had it been something to do with the alien on the enemy's side?

Merlin slowed his pace a little so that Wright caught up to him and Arthur walked ahead of them both. "I have to say, this time we've spent together has been somewhat eye-opening for me. Every so often, you say something impressively insightful."

"Well, thanks, but I'm not interested in impressing you. A simple answer to a straight question would be nice, though."

"Hmpf." Merlin didn't seem insulted. He studied the thin line of bare dirt they were following for a moment, then stooped and picked up a rock about the size of his fist. He held it up for Wright's perusal. "Tell me, Major. If you were to try to kill this stone, how would you go about it?"

"Kill the stone? What do you mean?"

"I mean, would you strangle it, shoot it, blow it up?"

"I suppose blowing it to pieces would destroy it."

"And would it be dead then?"

"No, it would just be separated into smaller fragments. You can't kill something that was never alive."

"This stone was never alive? Are you sure about that? Do you know what it's made from? What if it's limestone, formed originally from sea creatures?"

"From the non-living shells of sea creatures," Wright

corrected. "And even if it was kind of alive once, it isn't any longer."

"How do you know?"

"Because it doesn't move, reproduce, respirate…" he trailed off, trying to remember his biology lessons from when he was a kid.

"It doesn't meet the definition of a living organism, according to the criteria humans have decided."

"Yes."

Also, it's clearly not bloody alive.

"Are you confident those criteria are correct?" the alien asked.

Wright sighed, wishing he'd never begun the discussion. Maybe that was Merlin's intention—to confuse him and tie him up with semantics, distracting him from something important.

"You're saying we've got our definition of life wrong?" he replied. "Get to the point. Are you trying to tell me the rock's alive, but as a poor, dumb human I can't tell?"

"No." Merlin tossed the rock to the side of the trail. "What I'm trying to tell you, is that you might as well try to kill that piece of mineral as kill Dwyr Orr's companion."

He strode faster, rejoining Arthur's side and leaving Wright behind.

Wright had a brief vision of grabbing the rock, leaping on the alien's back, and smashing his head in with it.

He put the vision to one side.

32

Taylan opened her eyes. A little farther along the hedge, barely visible in the gap beneath it, Angharad's sons lay sleeping.

At least, she hoped they were asleep. The men had come back from planting the incendiaries more than an hour ago, and now they were supposed to be taking a short rest until just before dawn. Then, they would wake, slip closer to Bryn Celli Ddu, and set off the devices.

She'd deliberately chosen to sleep at a distance away from the men. Outwardly, she'd given the appearance of being sickened and saddened by what they were doing. *That* hadn't been hard to fake. But it had only been a ruse to explain her decision to physically separate from them. In fact, she wanted to be able to leave without notice when the time was right.

She wasn't only saddened because of what the brothers were doing, her heart felt heavy at the knowledge that this was where she would part ways from them. After what she was about to do, they would never accept her into their company again. If they saw her, they might even try to hurt her. She couldn't return to the hideout in the Preseli Hills. Her short time in the West BI Resistance was over.

She climbed slowly to her feet, trying to avoid making too much noise. The wind was strong, and the creaking and rustling of the hedge should cover the quiet sounds she was forced to make. She grabbed her nearly empty pack.

Keeping to the vegetation, she walked away from the sleeping men, planning on cutting over the fields when she couldn't be easily observed.

Footsteps sounded behind her.

She swung around. A figure loomed.

As her hand flew to her knife, the man said, "Taylan, it's only me."

Marc.

She relaxed. "I didn't recognize you. It's too dark. What are you doing?"

"I'm coming with you."

"No! You can't. Why?"

"You're going to remove the incendiaries, aren't you?"

Despite agreeing with her when she'd first mentioned her reservations about sabotaging the midsummer festival, Marc had gone with his brothers to plant the devices. She'd guessed that, when it came down to it, he hadn't wanted to stand up to the others. She hadn't blamed him. He was only young, about seventeen or eighteen.

"What I'm doing is none of your business," she retorted. "Go back and leave me alone." Speaking harshly to someone she liked so much was painful but necessary. She didn't want to be responsible for Marc provoking his brothers to hate him.

"I want to come with you. I don't agree with what they're doing. It's like you said, it would be wrong to hurt the children and babies. They haven't done anyone any harm."

"*Go back*, Marc." She strode away from him, worried that one of his siblings would wake up and see them.

He followed her, trotting at her side. "You don't know where we planted them. I do. I can take you to them, and we can remove them together."

It was true. She didn't know exactly where all the incendiaries were. She'd hoped to find them by guessing where *she* would have put them.

"And then what?" she asked. "What will you do then?"

"I'll sneak back. They'll never—"

"There isn't enough time. One of them is bound to wake up and notice you're gone. Then they'll see I've left too, and they'll put two and two together. Your brothers love you, but they'll never forgive you for this. I can manage by myself. I don't need you."

"You do. I'm telling you, you do. You'll never find them all. And I don't care if they find out I helped you."

"You *should* care. They're the only family you have left, and, believe me, you need to stick with your family, now more than ever. Don't make my mistake."

They'd walked a fair distance while they had their hurried, whispered conversation. Taylan estimated it was safe now to turn and head for the ancient mound. She had to get there soon. The Crusaders' camp was already stirring and a few people were wandering between the pavilions, even though none had opened yet. She was taking a risk of being challenged as it was.

"Marc, please. You're making this harder for me."

"Then stop arguing. I'm coming too, whether you like it or not."

She relented. What else could she do? He might be young, but he was tall and strong, taller and stronger than two of his brothers. She couldn't stop him from accompanying her if he insisted on it. And he was old enough to make his own decisions.

Without answering him, she turned and began to jog across

the rough grass. His boots thudded along with her on the soft, damp ground. The outlying pavilions drew closer.

"The nearest one is over there," said Mark, pointing at a candy-striped canopy. "Medwyn took care of that one. I'm not sure exactly where he put it."

There were probably quite a few places in the pavilions to hide a device. They were little bigger than Taylan's palm, flat and round and magnetized on one side. The enormity of what she was trying to do began to hit her. They'd brought thirty of them, and she only had a short time to find them all.

"Did you plant some on your own?" she asked.

"Yeah. I'll collect them first, then we can find the others."

"We should stop running," said Taylan. "It'll look suspicious."

They slowed to a walk. Trying her best to look like a freshly woken Crusader stretching her legs in an early morning stroll, she approached the outer edge of the pavilions with Marc.

"You're sure there's one in there?" she asked, nodding at the brightly colored canvas.

"Positive."

"Okay, I'll go and take a look. I suppose you should find the devices you hid," she added reluctantly. "But for god's sake be careful. I'll meet you south of the mound."

Marc loped away.

Taylan angled the direction of her walk to bring her close to her target. Its vivid hues were pale and grayish in the early morning light. Sounds of the wakening camp came to her on the breeze: babies crying to be fed, parents scolding children, someone chopping wood.

When she was within two meters of the pavilion, she took a quick look around to make sure she was unobserved, and then veered sharply left. Another quick survey, and she stepped between two overlapping edges of canvas.

In the dim interior, it was hard to figure out what was what.

As her eyes adjusted and her nose caught a familiar scent, she realized she was in a beer tent. Kegs were stacked behind a chest-high bar. Tall stools stood around similarly tall bar tables. The grass had been trampled flat and turned to sticky mud.

Where would Medwyn have hidden the incendiary? It had to be somewhere the servers and customers wouldn't usually have cause to look at.

She quickly inspected the undersides of the tables and stools. They were all bare. There was no point in searching among the kegs or glasses, she reasoned. When the workers arrived to set up, they would be the first places they would go.

She checked behind the bar, running a hand on the lower surface and peering into all the nooks and crannies.

Nothing.

She straightened up and turned a circle.

Where could it be?

Had Marc been wrong about Medwyn hiding a device in here?

Or had Marc been lying?

She halted.

Had the brothers anticipated her plan and persuaded him to trick her, to send her on a wild goose chase, wasting her time until they finally triggered the incendiaries?

It was possible, but she didn't believe it. Marc was too honest and decent.

Regardless, she had no choice except to carry on looking.

Medwyn hadn't felt any scruples about endangering the lives of the Crusaders. He would have put his device where it would be the most dangerous, where the fire would catch and spread quickly.

Her gaze rose.

The canvas.

After several days in the sun, the cloth was stiff and dry, and she doubted the EAC encouraged its people to use anything so technologically advanced as fire-retardant chemicals.

There it was!

At the junction of an upright strut and a roof support, a black, curved edge poked out. If she hadn't looked directly at it, she would never have noticed it. Grabbing a stool, she ran to the base of the strut. In another second she'd climbed up and lifted out the device.

One down. Twenty-nine to go.

33

———

Since the BA's global presence had dwindled, Lorcan had scaled down the armed personnel at the Kamboto Mine, as he had at many of his semi-legal and illegal operations around the world as a cost-saving measure. Consequently, when no guards had challenged him as he approached the mine in the rented car with Hale, he hadn't been too concerned. But when they got closer, up to the fence around the site, and there was no sign of even a security team, his anger had begun to boil.

Traveling with Hale and hearing her constant criticism was bad enough, but his experience at Kamboto had topped even that. He was relieved to be finally on his way back to the *Bres*, though he had plenty of work to do. The cobalt mine had been an example of what happened when he took his eye off the ball for too long. He'd been distracted by Hale's interference in the Project. That was his biggest problem, but he couldn't do anything about it.

He recalled the mine manager's widening eyes and gaping mouth as he appeared in her dirty little office, Hale trailing him. What an annoying, obsequious woman she'd been. But no amount of creeping and obfuscating could hide the facts.

Mining had been Lorcan's business from the early days. It was what he'd built his empire on. And he was not so out of touch that he couldn't tell at a glance what should be happening, where, how, and using what equipment.

After a lot of feet-dragging and excuses, the manager had finally agreed to a snap inspection. With a surly look and her shoulder's hunched, she'd escorted them to the elevator shaft and taken them below ground. Lorcan had insisted on seeing *everything*.

The woman had been cutting corners and bending rules with an arrogant flagrancy that shocked him, seasoned though he was in his experience of the business.

He'd seen a boy of perhaps twelve or thirteen standing at a ventilation shaft, operating a fan.

Processes that should have been automated were being carried out by children.

A temporary measure, until I can get it fixed, the manager had spluttered. *The younger the laborers, the cheaper they are. I barely have to pay them anything at all.*

Lorcan couldn't remember what he'd said. A red rage had descended on him. He might have struck the woman. He simply couldn't recall his actions. What he did remember was Hale screaming at him to calm down.

Temporary measure! It had been a blatant lie. Why pay a qualified engineer for a repair or invest in new machinery when you could pay a kid a pittance?

Yet, reflecting on the incident as the shuttle flew to the *Bres*, he understood what had affected him most hadn't been the bare-faced lying of the manager or her pathetic cost-cutting excuses, or even the danger created by her stupidity and neglect, it had been how the boy reminded him of his own...

His lips thinned to a line and he looked out the window, not seeing anything of the starscape or the distant corkscrew of the *Bres*. The old, old wound never seemed to heal, no matter how many years passed or how much he thought or didn't think about what had happened and the family he'd lost.

Hale and Camilla were talking, and gradually their conversation infiltrated his thoughts. Camilla was relating a story about a cousin who had become a net celebrity by promoting healing with colored water.

"He dyes the water different hues depending on the ailment, saying the colors give off vibrations and he has to achieve exactly the right set of vibrations for the treatment to work. The patients are supposed to immerse themselves naked for hours at a time. Of course, if it doesn't work, it's because the patient lacks faith in the process and their negative vibrations are affecting it."

"Of course," said Hale. "Do you know how much money he's making?"

"No, but it's a lot."

"Looks like we have another Dwyr Orr on our hands."

"I certainly hope not." Camilla turned to Lorcan. "You might receive an application from him any day now. He's got the creds for a ticket to a new world. I'm sure of it."

"He'll need it to get away from all his disappointed clients," Hale said, "when they finally come after him."

"Oh, I'm sure they won't," Camilla replied. "You know what people are like. They'll just keep sending him money, hoping it'll work one day. Or they'll find another quack to follow."

"Did you say anything to him?" asked Hale.

"No. What's the point? He seems to believe in it himself. Either that, or he's a good faker."

"Thanks for the heads up," said Lorcan. "Let me know his name and I'll be sure to screen him out. The last thing we'll need in the colony is a snake oil salesman."

"If you think you'll be able to screen them all out," Hale

said, "you're going to be disappointed. Believing in nonsense is part of human nature."

"I suppose you're right," he replied.

She seemed to have softened toward him a little bit since their time at the mine. Maybe she'd come to accept he wasn't quite the monster she'd thought.

"I only wish *you* would agree to come along," he told her. They'd been through a lot, and some days he couldn't bear the sight of her, but that hadn't dulled his perception that she would be a huge asset on a new world. "The offer remains open, you know."

"You never give up, do you?"

"You can't blame me for trying." He gave her a half smile.

"How do you feel about your other scientists, Lorcan?" asked Camilla. "Are we welcome to accompany you on the Project too?"

Camilla had a cheeky look in her eye. He couldn't tell if she was joking. After Hale's blank refusal, it hadn't occurred to him to propose that Camilla and Anders joined the colony expedition.

"Naturally," he replied. "You would be very welcome. Free of charge."

"Now there's an offer I might find hard to refuse!"

"Landing in five minutes," said the pilot over the comm.

A tiny spark of warm hope flared in Lorcan's heart. Camilla Lebedev aboard the *Bres* as she set out on her great voyage? It would be a pleasure he hadn't anticipated. He enjoyed her company immensely. She was extremely intelligent, witty, cultured, and affable. She had none of Hale's sharp corners, and, like Hale, her input would be invaluable.

He'd found the visit to the Kamboto mine deeply depressing and unsettling, but things were looking up. The Project was back on track and more poised for success than ever now that top scientists were ironing out some of the wrinkles.

Lorcan straightened up and fastened his seat belt.

THE FIRST THING he saw as he disembarked in the *Bres's* bay was Anders, waiting at the entrance. He'd remained behind, continuing to work while the others had their excursion on the surface. Lorcan was mildly alarmed when he saw him.

Had something gone wrong? Had the man discovered a fatal flaw in the Project?

But then he noticed that Anders wasn't looking at him. He was peering at a spot behind him—the shuttle hatch. When Camilla and Hale stepped out, his expression brightened and he began to walk toward them.

"Good trip?" he asked Lorcan.

Before he could reply, Anders raised his arms and stepped past him.

"Darling," he said. "I missed you."

He was embracing Camilla.

Lorcan felt his mouth drop open.

Noticing his surprise, Iolani took his arm and led him away. "They're married," she said softly. "Didn't you know?"

"No." He had the uncomfortable sensation of something slipping away from him. He frowned. "But they have separate cabins."

"Yes, Anders snores like an elephant, and they have completely different working habits. Back on Earth, they lived next door to each other." She gave him a sympathetic look. "Sorry if that was a shock."

"No, no," he said, struggling to regain his composure. "Their private lives are their own business. I'm just a bit surprised, that's all. It doesn't change anything."

"Good. Because I need to talk to you about something else. I could tell the visit to the Kamboto mine disturbed you, and we couldn't talk on the shuttle with Camilla around…"

He suppressed a groan. What was Hale going to harp on about now? He'd fixed the problem at the mine. If this was more rubbish about asteroid mining…

"You really need to help the Britannic Alliance."

"*What*?! Why on Earth, or in space, would I help *them*?" For most of the duration of the Project, the Alliance had been hampering his efforts. And the one time he'd helped them out of dire situation, he hadn't received any recompense or gratitude.

"If you do manage to leave the Solar System in the next few years," said Hale, "imagine what you'll be leaving behind. If the EAC get control, it'll throw the whole place back into the Dark Ages."

"One, what makes you so sure the BA needs my help? The latest on the vidnews is they've taken back the Caribbean. And, two, why should I care about the state of the world I'm leaving behind? People are free to choose to follow a cult, and they're free to live with the consequences of their decisions."

"Lorcan, you know as well as I do the Alliance is spread too thin. Other powers are either too weak, too mired in petty wars, or too apathetic to mount an adequate defense to the Dwyr if she gets her act together. I admit she does seem distracted lately, but that could change anytime. As to your second point, do you really want to see our home planet reduced to a pre-Enlightenment, anti-intellectual wasteland? And if that doesn't sway you, think of this: what if the Project fails? What if the ships' engines don't work as well as you expect, or humans can't survive cryosuspension, or you can't find anywhere suitable for colonization, and you have to come home? With Dwyr Orr running everything, think about what kind of Earth you'll find on your return."

34

Taylan only waited a short while for Marc to meet her south of Bryn Celli Ddu. He was grinning as he trotted toward her, his pockets bulging with incendiary devices. She remained conflicted about involving him in her scheme to prevent his brothers from sabotaging the ceremony, but she didn't feel she had a lot of choice about it.

"That was quick," she said.

"It's easy to be fast when you know exactly where they are." He gave her the devices he'd collected and she put them in her pack, deactivating each one as she did so.

"Let's find the others," she said. "We don't have much time."

The sky had brightened even as she'd waited for him, and the number of early arrivals was increasing. The people running the refreshment and entertainment areas would be among them as they would be setting up for the long day ahead.

"Meilyr planted one over there," said Marc. "In the admissions tent."

A small booth stood next to a gap in the rope barrier surrounding the ancient mound. It seemed that a select few

Crusaders would be allowed inside the mound itself to witness the sun's beams striking the inner stone. They would probably show something to an attendant in the booth before passing inside. Meilyr's choice would create a devastating effect if the device went off and would probably kill whoever stood inside the small tent at the time. The incendiaries spat a highly flammable, clinging oil when they were triggered.

Someone was approaching the tent.

"You grab it," said Marc. "I'll distract them."

"No, it's too dangerous," Taylan protested.

But he was already on his way, adopting a trajectory that would cross the Crusader's path.

She fast-walked to the small booth, her head down, trying to not look conspicuous. As she reached it, from the corners of her eyes, she saw Marc 'accidentally' collide with the man. She slipped in the back.

Her gaze quickly roved every surface. The place was almost bare. Just a table, a couple of chairs, some open-topped, empty boxes... She scanned the ceiling in case Meilyr had taken a leaf from Medwyn's book, but the frame was empty.

From outside came the strains of a conversation.

Marc, talking to the Crusader!

Her stomach twisted into knots. He was taking a huge risk. If his fake accent slipped, the man would realize he wasn't one of them. Marc had always been cocky about his ability to mimic Crusader talk, making fun of them to entertain the Resistance fighters. Too cocky.

She turned, about to step outside and attract his attention, to extract him from the dangerous conversation, when her boot hit something solid. Beneath one of the chairs was a metal, cylindrical container. Maybe somewhere to put trash. She opened the lid, but it was empty. She lifted it and tipped it upside down. The black incendiary clung to the underside.

She tore it off, threw down the container, and darted out.

Marc and the Crusader were still talking.

Jumping up, she waved her arms. Marc saw her and ended his conversation with a nod and a smile.

"What on Earth are you doing?" Taylan hissed when he reached her.

"It's fine. He didn't suspect a thing. And if I hadn't delayed him, he would have discovered you searching the tent for sure. Did you find it?"

"Yes, I did, but don't do that again, okay? I might want to prevent the people here from being hurt, but you mean more to me than them. If you find you have to take that level of risk again, I want you to bail. I can look after myself."

"Meilyr put another one in that guards' hut," he said.

Gritting her teeth at his failure to acknowledge what she'd said, she replied, "He did? That was some feat." Guards could be seen moving about inside the little wooden building. "Was it empty at the time?"

"I'm not sure. He might have hidden it in the grass on the outside."

"We'll leave that one. The guards can look after themselves." Anyone carrying a weapon was fair game as far as she was concerned.

"All right. Madog put a couple in that big marquee. The one that looks like it's set up for shows."

She could see the one he meant. An open-fronted structure, it was covered by cloth bearing odd symbols and designs. "Okay, let's see if we can find them."

They did. Madog had hidden the incendiaries in amongst a pile of acting equipment. They were easily visible in the costumes and props, but he must have predicted no one would be using them until later in the day. Certainly, the miscellaneous items would create quite a conflagration.

The noises of the gathering crowd were growing louder.

They hadn't collected even half the devices yet. They were running out of time.

"We have to go faster," said Marc. "It won't be long before my brothers are here with the remote detonator. They've probably already woken up and noticed we're missing."

He was right. The damage to his relationship with his brothers was done by now, and Taylan's heart ached with regret. The last thing she'd wanted to do was drive a wedge between them.

"We'll have to accept we won't get them all," she said. "We'll get as many as we can, then leave before sunup." That was the moment Meilyr would set off the incendiaries.

It was a clear morning, and the patch of sky where the sun would rise was glowing faintly golden.

"Where do we go next?" she asked.

"Uh..." he peered around the site "yeah, this way."

She followed him.

Over the next fifteen minutes, they gathered another six devices. But the crowd was growing so thick it was becoming a crush and Taylan felt extremely vulnerable. They had attracted some curious glances, and she couldn't speak with a Crusader accent like Marc could.

"Okay," she said, thrusting an incendiary into her pack as they stood at the back of a pavilion, "we're done. Let's go."

"No, we have time to get a couple more," said Marc. "It's at least ten minutes until sunrise."

"It's less than that, and even if we did have ten minutes, it's still too risky. We need to get out of here before the incendiaries we didn't get go off. When that happens, the Crusaders will be looking for someone to blame, and we stand out too much."

"Just one more, then. I remembered there's one really close by. It'll only take—"

"No!"

But after a second's hesitation, he left her, striding away through the crowd.

"Marc!" she called, then immediately cringed as people looked in her direction.

"Marc," she whispered.

Dammit.

She took off after him.

Beyond the edge of the crowd, in the green fields that led to the hedgerows, walked three tall, dark-haired men. They would have been noticeable if anyone had been taking any notice. But the Crusaders were fixated on what was about to happen. Throngs of people were making their way closer to Bryn Celli Ddu, hastening to be near the sacred site as the midsummer sun breasted the horizon.

Where was Marc?

She'd taken her eyes off him for a moment and now she couldn't see him. There were too many people about.

He was cutting it too fine. Meilyr and the others were on their way. They had to have guessed she and Marc had been removing the incendiaries. Would they try to set them off regardless, knowing the risks?

Where are you, you stupid kid?

She rushed forward.

A woman bumped into her. "Watch out! Be more careful." The woman pulled her shawl tighter and hurried on her way.

The murmuring of the crowd was growing louder. Crusaders surged around the mound like waves on a stormy night. All heads faced one direction: east.

Taylan didn't hear the incendiaries go off. What she heard first was a scream.

Then there was a shout, louder than the chattering hum of the masses of people.

"FIRE!"

But someone else was screaming, shrieking in agony.

Taylan flew toward the noise, knocking aside everyone in her way.

A figure stumbled from a pavilion, engulfed in flames. She threw herself on him, wrapping him in her arms, rolling over and over on the wet grass. But the fire wouldn't go out. It clung to her, searing her. She smelled her hair burning.

She was vaguely aware of people surrounding them, gawping in horror, and, farther off, cries of alarm and horror.

Why didn't someone do something? Were they just going to let them burn?

Something heavy landed on her, something wide and soft that covered her and Marc entirely, turning the world dark. Hands pressed down. The blanket was smothering her. She couldn't breathe. But the flames had been extinguished.

She was still holding Marc. Squirming in her arms, he moaned in pain.

35

———————

Hans had been watching the harbor for several days, watching and waiting. Leaving Jamaica had proven harder than he'd thought it would be. Much to his surprise, he'd seen posters bearing his face appear around Kingston, stating that anyone knowing his whereabouts was to report to the country's interim government, the Resistance leaders.

Luckily, the only image they had of him was from his days as Head of SIS. His appearance had altered considerably since then.

What had surprised him was the vindictiveness of Charles, Devon, and the rest of them in seeking him out after he'd disappeared. It was as if they were looking for someone to blame for the state of things. No one was to blame. It was just that circumstances weren't right for what they wanted to achieve.

They'd aimed too high, been too unrealistic. They had to walk before they could run, but they wouldn't have listened if he'd tried to tell them.

He hugged his cloth bag to his chest as he squatted in the

bushes that fringed the quay. He needed to take his next step very carefully. If he got it wrong, he would be given up to the Resistance or his throat would be cut and he would be dumped in the sea. The wealth he was holding was more than the fishermen could expect to earn over several lifetimes. He needed someone willing to take him off the island for a generous fee, but not so corrupt as to kill him for whatever else he might be carrying.

The harbor side was busy as the ships' captains and crews arrived and prepared the boats for that night's fishing. Vessels of all kinds bobbed in the water, from massive, automated, commercial shrimpers to small, independent boats that probably fished whatever they could find in the rapidly depleting seas.

Of all the people who frequented the place, Hans had focused on an older woman who fished alone. She seemed to mostly catch lobsters and crabs, going out daily to haul the pots and refresh the bait. She was friendly with all the folk she met but she kept to herself. Her age and gender made her less likely to murder him, he hoped, while she looked poor enough to be tempted to help a wanted man for a reward.

It was about the time she was due to return with that day's catch.

Hans shifted a little to ease his aching muscles.

Was that her? A smallish boat was heading for the harbor, its engine loud despite the distance.

It was her.

He stood and lifted the strap of his bag over his head so it sat across his chest. After several days living rough, he stank. He hated being dirty almost as much as he hated being hungry and thirsty and having nowhere comfortable to sleep. But perhaps his situation was about to change.

When the boat had softly bumped into the harbor wall and

the woman had climbed out to secure it with loops of rope, Hans stepped from his hiding place.

Checking that no one was looking his way, he crossed the stone quayside and went up to her. She was bending over a cleat. She saw his shoes first. Her gaze traveled up his body to his face. She stared at him blankly.

Good. She hadn't recognized him from the posters.

"I'm sorry to bother you, but I'm looking for someone to take me... I'll be frank. I need a boat to take me out of the Caribbean. But if that's too far for your liking, passage to another island would be sufficient."

The woman straightened up and put a hand on her hip. She glanced behind her and all around before replying, "You talking to me?"

"Yes. I can pay, of course, though not in creds. Gold. These days, I'd say that was a more reliable currency, wouldn't you?"

"You want me to what?"

"I'd like for you to take me off Jamaica. Now. I know you've only just brought in your catch, but I can compensate you for whatever it's worth." His nerves were starting to get to him. If they continued talking much longer, someone was bound to wonder what was happening and come over to find out.

"If the answer's no, that's fine, but I need you to decide."

She held eye contact with him, unblinking.

"I can see I've taken up enough of your time," said Hans, turning.

"No, no, no," she objected. "Where you going? I'm still thinking."

Tense with stress, he faced her again.

"You wanna get off t' island?"

"I do," he agreed, adding unnecessarily, "That's exactly what I want."

"Hey, Hester!" someone shouted. "You have a good day?"

Ignoring the man, she said to Hans, "Watchyu waiting for? Come aboard." She began to unhitch the ropes.

Paradoxically, a fresh outpouring of sweat coated him as he relaxed, finally assured he would escape. He grabbed the bow of the boat for security and swung a leg over the side.

"Wait a minute," said Hester. "I wanna see that gold 'for we set off."

"No problem." Hans dug into his pocket and produced the three solid gold antique coins he'd put there to avoid revealing his hoard.

Hester's eyebrows rose and she held out her hand, palm upward. Hans placed one of the coins on it. She bit the shiny metal and inspected the dent while Hans had the strangest feeling he was in a holodrama. After tucking the coin into a strip of cloth wrapped around her waist, she continued to untie the rope.

"Who's tat fella?" her acquaintance asked, coming closer. He was a tall fellow in his later years, more bones and skin than meat, and gap-toothed. "He your boyfriend? I'm jealous."

Hester replied in Patois, telling him to shut up and mind his own business.

Hans sat in the stern of the boat and watched, concerned the newcomer would attract more attention and someone might recognize him.

The man didn't leave, however. His expression switched from mild curiosity and amusement to a keener interest. Narrowing his eyes, he scrutinized Hans, who wished he could flip over the side of the boat like a scuba diver. But there was nothing he could do except wait for his ride to finish completing her slow preparations to leave.

She was done. She climbed into her vessel with surprising nimbleness for her age and started the engine.

The old man on the quay beckoned the other fishermen and invited them to come and see Hester's new boyfriend. He sounded like he was joking, but Hans detected a layer of suspicion and excitement beneath his words.

Hester piloted her boat in a curve, taking them out to sea.

Her gaze on the water, she shouted over the noisy engine, "You're that man in the posters, right?"

His chest tightened. "I...er..."

There was no point in denying it. Hester had guessed the truth, yet she was helping him anyway.

"I am," he said. "I hope that isn't a problem."

She thrust out her lower lip as she considered.

"No, it don't matter," she said in the end. "I mind my business and no one else's. It's the best way." She smiled a lazy smile.

Hans did a double take. Reaching into his shirt pocket, he pulled out a photograph and looked at it before regarding Hester again.

"Tell me," he said, "do you have any children?"

"No, I been single all my life. Why you asking?"

"It's not important."

He watched the green island shrinking as the boat drew away.

A ship's engine noisier than Hester's attracted his attention in the opposite direction. A gleaming white ship was parting the waves, sea foam streaming from her prow.

An Alliance battleship.

The Jamaican Resistance had caved and accepted BA help. In return, they'd given up their country's independence.

36

I t was dusk, three days after midsummer, and Wright was watching Merlin as he settled down crossed-legged on a high hilltop. The alien closed his eyes and breathed in deeply. Meanwhile, Arthur wandered to a drop and stood at the edge, hand on sword hilt.

Wright would have objected to the alien's decision to go to this exposed location, but they were in the middle of nowhere. Despite their high elevation, no buildings were visible as far as the eye could see and they hadn't encountered another soul since yesterday morning when they'd spied someone riding a trail bike in the distance.

Ellis would be coming back from the festival and they had to find her before she passed them on her way to the Preseli Hills hideout. In the vast tracts of wild, mountainous country-side it seemed an impossible feat, but Merlin appeared confident they would do it. He'd mentioned something about 'patterns converging' and things 'playing out'.

Arthur had simply accepted the alien's pronouncements and followed him like a shaggy dog—a dog that could turn vicious in the right circumstances. Wright had felt powerless to do anything else except go along too. He did hope they could find Ellis, though he hated the prospect of persuading her to return with him to the *Gallant* and carry out Merlin's plan. It would be good to see her again.

He found an area of flat outcrop and sat on it, wondering how long the alien would take to home in on Ellis, if that was what he was doing. He could be communicating with his extra-terrestrial masters for all anyone knew, sending them a message that said Earth civilizations were so busy warring with each other the planet was ripe for taking.

He rubbed the top of his head. At that lofty position, the wind blew strong and cool, finding every entry point in his clothes. To pass the time, he opened his pack and checked his supplies. Another couple of days of food was all that remained. Water was easy to find but they would start feeling hungry soon. Arthur had supplemented their diet with rabbits, but he hadn't had time to trap many and the animals had no fat and little meat on them. It was a good thing the alien ate nothing.

After watching the darkening landscape for twenty minutes, he grew cold and stiff. He stood up and stretched. Merlin hadn't changed position, but Arthur had disappeared. Wright walked to the drop and peered over it. He couldn't see any sign of the king among the rough scrub that clung to the steep slope.

"I think I may have found her."

Wright nearly leapt off the precipice. "Don't sneak up on me like that!" he scolded Merlin, whose soft voice he'd heard next to his ear.

"But we'll have to be quick," the alien went on as if Wright hadn't spoken. "She's already passed us, and she'll be hard to see in the dark."

"Great. Where's Arthur?"

As he spoke, the king's figure appeared striding into sight at the other end of the hilltop. "Do you have her, Merlin? I spied out an obvious route through the hills. We've been making things hard for ourselves, taking a difficult path."

"Excellent," the alien replied. "Do you see what I mean now about patterns converging, Major?"

Wright grunted a response.

"We need to descend this way," Arthur said.

They followed a thread-like trail down the high hill, made even harder to discern by the rapid failing of the light. It was a starry night, but the moon hadn't risen yet. Merlin went first, setting a rapid pace. Wright wondered how far they had to go to catch up to Ellis and what he would say if they did find her somehow.

At the foot of the hill Arthur took the lead and walked no less quickly than Merlin. Wright was last in the line of three, as had become the norm over the days they had spent together. He struggled a little to keep up, partly because he was already tired from the day's trek, and partly because reluctance was dragging at his feet.

They traversed the valley, passing the hills on each side. Wright began to lose his sense of time passing. His world narrowed down to the almost-invisible track, the two men ahead of him, and the slowly wheeling stars above. Every so often Arthur would call out things like, *This way* and *I think we go left here* but otherwise no one spoke.

Then Wright heard Merlin mutter, "I hope we haven't missed her." A moment later he said, louder, "Arthur, are you sure we haven't lost our way?"

"I don't think so," came the king's reply. "Should we stop and shout for her? The hills will carry the echo, and I doubt there are any enemies about."

"No," said Wright. "It's too dangerous, even out here. I say we continue walking. She might be nowhere near—"

"Major Wright?" asked a soft, female voice.

Someone stepped out from the shadows between rocks on the side of the trail.

"Taylan!" Arthur exclaimed. "We found you at last."

He stepped closer to her, but she shrank from his approach and took a small detour around him to reach Wright. "I heard people coming down the track. I never guessed it would be you."

"Ellis." His first impulse was to hug her but that wouldn't be appropriate. Also, she was hunched over. "Are you okay?"

"Not really. What are you all doing? And how the hell did you find me? Has Colbourn been tracking my implant?"

"No, that wouldn't be safe."

"You're telling me!"

"Are you..." Wright peered at her face, half-hidden by her hood. "Have you been hurt?"

"Yeah, but you still haven't told me what you're doing here. Have you really come all this way just to find me?"

"It'll take a while to explain. Let's make camp somewhere and I'll lay it out for you."

Ellis looked at Arthur and Merlin, appearing uncertain. She clearly hadn't forgotten her changed impression of the king, and she'd never liked the alien. Wright realized she hadn't revealed herself until after *he'd* spoken, though she must have recognized all their voices. She wouldn't have come out of her hiding place if it had been only the other two.

"Can't you give me the short version?" she asked.

Merlin wants you to help us try to kill the Dwyr again.

That was the short version, but if he told her that, she'd probably unleash the same response she'd given Colbourn via comm. "I'd prefer it if we could talk for a while. Do you need food? We have some to share, though it's not much."

"I have plenty of food." She sighed, and he caught a flash of cool gray eyes meeting his gaze. "All right. I suppose it won't hurt to hear you out."

As they walked to find a spot suitable to spend the night, Wright noticed Taylan was moving as though she was in pain. Then, when they sat down together he got a better look at her face.

He gasped.

The right-hand side of it was blistered, swollen, and weeping, and her right eye was only partially open. And though he couldn't see well under her hood, it seemed her hair on that side had been burned to her scalp.

"What happened to you?"

"That's another long explanation. Let's do yours first."

"Taylan, you must be in pain," said Arthur. "Let Merlin heal you before we talk."

She hesitated. "No, I'll be okay."

"Those are third-degree burns, Ellis," said Wright. "If you don't have them treated they'll get infected. I don't know how you can walk around with an injury like that."

She gave a slight smile, and he understood he'd put on his 'major' voice.

"I want to hear what you have to say," she said.

He silently cursed, though he couldn't blame her for insisting. He had a feeling the moment he told her Merlin's plan, that would be the last he would see of her.

"Okay, but hear me out before you come to a decision. And even if you don't like what I have to say, promise me you'll stay with us tonight and let us help you."

"No, I'm not promising anything." She glanced at Merlin and Arthur.

Oh well. He'd tried his best.

He told her about the proposal to cloak the *Gallant* and approach the Dwyr's flagship with the intention of boarding it and assassinating her. He left out the part about it being

Merlin's idea. There was no point in making it even more likely that Ellis would refuse.

To his surprise, she didn't immediately say no.

Another thing struck him: she clearly hadn't found her children. He was sure she wouldn't have undertaken the attempt to sabotage the Crusader's festival if that had been the case.

"What happened at the midsummer celebration?" he asked.

"I'd rather not talk about it."

"It didn't work out?"

Ignoring his question, she said, "This plan of yours, I'm prepared to consider it, but on one condition."

37

Kala was determined to not make the same mistake twice. She'd asked the *Belladonna's* chief medical officer to supply her with sedatives, claiming she found it hard to sleep. That had been easy. Crushing up a couple of the tablets and mixing them into Perran's evening drink had been harder, but she'd managed it without him or Morgan noticing. The drug would take effect slowly, but once her son was asleep, he wouldn't wake for another seven or eight hours, no matter what.

By then, she hoped to be far from her usurper's sphere of influence.

All she needed was for the rest of her efforts over the last couple of weeks to bear fruit.

Luckily, Morgan hadn't restricted her movements around the ship or removed her security access. Perhaps she underestimated Kala or was uninterested in how things worked aboard the starship.

Lying in bed waiting for the hours to pass was the hardest part. Kala's muscles ached with tension. This might be her only and final chance to outwit Morgan. If she failed, who knew what the woman would do in retaliation this time around? But what choice did she have? She couldn't live under another's rule. She'd spent her entire life ensuring *she* was the one with the power, the one in control. She couldn't allow another to stand in her way. Her entire being rebelled against the notion.

It was time.

As she had before on her first attempt to leave, she rose and went silently to Perran's cabin. She'd worked out the best route for avoiding other people. She mostly trusted her crew, who seemed to remain loyal to her whenever Morgan wasn't around, but she couldn't take even the smallest risk.

Perran lay with his mouth open, sleeping heavily. She didn't waste time gathering any of his belongings. He would probably complain about it when he woke up but she would find a way to mollify him. Enduring his anger and disappointment when he realized she'd taken him away from Morgan was a small price to pay for their freedom from the tyrant.

She uncovered him and slipped her arms under his sleeping form. With some difficulty, she lifted him and put him over her shoulder to help support his weight. It had been several years since she'd carried him like this. The feeling brought back happy memories of him as a small boy, when he'd been young enough to sit on her lap and cuddle her.

Something in her heart seemed to twist and she found herself swallowing tears.

She would *not* allow that bitch to take her son from her.

His cabin door slid aside and she carried him into the passageway.

Selecting and preparing the crew members who would help her had been a long and difficult process. First, she had to approach the person in question while Morgan was not around. This had proven hard to do because Morgan had insisted they spent most of their time together. Not that she'd continued to instruct Kala in the skills she possessed. No, that privilege was now reserved for Perran only. Instead, Morgan had seemed to take a special pleasure in forcing her to attend her son's lessons and witness a process that was now off limits to her.

Consequently, she'd spent little time alone.

Next, she'd had to subtly question them to assess whether they would be able or willing to help her. This had been where she'd feared things going wrong the most. All it would have taken was one of the people she'd approached to tell Morgan what she was attempting, and she would have found herself back in the brig, or worse.

Then, she'd put together the steps of her escape and relayed the information to the trusted individuals. The harrowing procedure had taken weeks.

The shuttle bay hatch appeared in the passageway ahead of her. She'd managed to reach it without encountering anyone else. Her co-conspirators had kept her path empty.

The hatch opened at her approach. No problems with a security lockout.

Wonderful.

Finding a pilot to take her to Earth had been nearly impossible, unsurprisingly given what had happened to the last one. Eventually, an older man who had worked for her for years had agreed. She had yet to think of a worthy reward for him when they reached their destination, but it would be something highly valuable, plus a sizable pension.

The pilot waited outside the shuttlecraft as instructed. She wasn't going to take the same risk as before. When she and Perran were ready, he would step inside and start the engines. Then she would fly to freedom.

She climbed aboard and put Perran down in the nearest seat, quickly fastening his seat belt. She checked the pilot's cabin. It was empty.

"It's safe," she called out to him before taking a seat herself.

As she strapped in, she heard the pilot's door close. A soft rumble coursed through the vessel as the engines fired.

Just another couple of minutes. She could hardly believe she was nearly free.

The shuttle lifted and hung in midair for a second, then she felt gentle pressure as it moved forward. The bay bulkheads passed by on each side. Black space appeared, speckled with the hard, silver points of stars.

She'd done it. They were away. Unless Morgan realized she'd escaped in the next hour or so, she would find it hard to come after her. And would she want to risk a battle with Perran aboard the shuttle? Kala didn't think so. Perran was the last of her descendants. She wouldn't want to risk hurting him.

Kala relaxed and looked at her sleeping son. He would get over not seeing Morgan anymore. He'd only known her a few months. And she would make sure to spoil him to help him forget.

She'd decided to return to the castle she'd lived at before her most recent habitation. Morgan had never been there. She'd never met any of the staff and so hadn't had the opportunity to influence them. It was conceivable that she would try to raise an army to attack her, but outside of Kala's immediate retinue, hardly anyone in the EAC had seen her. She had no reputation, no influence other than over people in her immediate vicinity, and little experience of the world. She might be hard to kill—Kala hadn't given up on her plan to discover Morgan's enemy—but that didn't mean she was to be feared forever. She might only continue as an impotent irritation, a gnat to be swatted away when she got too close.

Kala closed her eyes as her tension eased some more. She'd been on edge for weeks. Telling the doctor she was unable to sleep had been no lie. She breathed deeply and focused on the smooth motion of the shuttle as it carried her away from her deadly foe.

A short time later, she opened her eyes again.

On darkness.

She jerked to full awareness, her eyes stretching wide.

Why was it dark?

In her panic, she grabbed her armrests, but there was nothing for her to hold. Her seat had disappeared too. She was floating without support in a void.

"Pilot!"

"Pilot, answer me!"

Silence.

"Perran! Perran! Where are you?"

She reached out but her hands met nothing. Her feet did the same.

Where was she? Where had the shuttle gone? Where was Perran?

Was she dreaming?

An icy claw of fear clutching her heart, she prayed it was only a nightmare, that she would wake up aboard the *Belladonna*, her escape plan still in place.

On the edge of her hearing, she heard a soft, familiar chuckle.

38

———

Taylan watched Merlin and Arthur disappear into the night. When she couldn't see them anymore, she said to Wright, "I never thought he would agree to it."

"Merlin? He badly wants to carry out his plan, for some reason. I'm not sure why. Ooops." He gave her a sheepish look.

"It's okay. I'd already figured out this was all his idea. I didn't think you liked me so much you would trek for days through the wilds of West BI, enemy territory, just to find me."

Now he looked a little hurt. "What makes you think I don't like you? I wasn't that bad a CO to you, was I?"

"No, that isn't what I meant. You have to admit, this is excessive. There has to be a thousand other Marines who would be just as good as me at trying to take out the Dwyr."

"Not a thousand. A hundred, maybe. Ten at least."

She smiled, then winced and raised her hand to the side of her face.

"I wish you'd let Merlin treat you before he left."

She shook her head, and then winced again. "*I* wish I would stop doing that."

"You must be in a lot of pain. Hey, I forgot. I brought along some meds." He fished in his pack and handed her a strip of blisters that was nearly empty.

"But you've been using these," she said. "You must need them. I can't take them."

"I don't need them as much as you do. Go on, please. It would make me feel better."

Her burns did hurt like a bitch, keeping her awake at night and making every movement painful. She popped one of the pills and swallowed it with a sip of water.

"No luck with your kids?" he asked quietly.

About to shake her head again, she remembered just in time. "No."

There was so much more she could have told him on that front, about spying on the orphanage and getting shot, and her guess that Patrin and Kayla might have been taken in by a Crusader couple. But she didn't think she could do it. "No luck," was all she could manage.

He got the hint and didn't press her to tell him more. "How long do you think it'll be before Arthur and Merlin come back?"

"Uhh, about a day, day and a half." She'd set out at the same time as the brothers, but they were moving much slower than her due to carrying Marc on a stretcher.

It had been an enormous relief when Merlin had agreed to heal Marc in return for her participation in the mission. The guilt of his injuries had weighed heavy on her, even though he'd insisted on helping her remove the incendiaries. If she hadn't been at the festival and objected to the sabotage, he wouldn't have got hurt. He'd been fortunate to survive the horrible burns from the device going off in his hands. He could easily have died and she would have had to live with the fact for the rest of her days. She had plenty of regrets already without adding another to the list.

"It looks like we have quite a wait ahead of us," said Wright.

"Are you hungry? Do you want to eat something? I could start a fire if you're cold, too. I think it'll be safe out here."

Now that the meds were taking effect, she had felt her appetite begin to return. "I have lots of food." She hadn't touched her supplies since leaving Ynys Mon. "You should have some of mine. And a fire would be great."

As the major went to gather wood, she took out some of the parcels the Crusaders had given her and opened them. She found strips of preserved meat, dried fruit, savory biscuits, some kind of confectionery, and nuts in their shells. The people had been so kind and generous, the memory of them filling her pack before she set off brought tears to her eyes.

It had been so odd. They hadn't seemed to guess she and Marc might have had something to do with the fires that had simultaneously broken out at the festival site. Marc being a victim of one of the fires probably had something to do with that. They hadn't appeared to recognize the deactivated incendiaries in her pack, perhaps unremarkably if anyone who saw them had no military experience.

Retrieving the majority of the devices had meant the few fires that started up were dealt with before things got out of control. She and Marc had prevented a terrible disaster, so that was something to be grateful for. But Marc had suffered horribly and she'd lost Meilyr and Madog's friendship forever. Not Medwyn's. He'd never liked her anyway. Regarding the other two, if they'd felt animosity toward her because she'd upset their plans, involving their brother so he was left severely burned had put the seal on it. She would never be able to look either of them in the eyes again.

Wright walked into the campsite and dropped a bundle of sticks. "There's plenty of wood about. We should have enough to keep a fire going all night." With that, he set off to find some more. When he returned and added to the bundle, he started a small fire.

"Here," she said, "have one of these." She handed him a candy and popped one in her own mouth too. "What do you think it is?"

He chewed. "No idea. Is it a West BI specialty?"

"No, I got it from a Crusader."

"You're kidding?! How come?"

"Sit down. I'll tell you what happened at the festival."

When he was sitting next to her, she asked, "What do I call you now?"

"Huh?"

"Unless you still want me to call you Major Wright."

"Oh, T.J. will do."

"*T.J.* That's it. That's what Arthur calls you. What do the initials stand for?"

"Nothing very interesting."

"Don't worry, you can tell me. Is it something embarrassing?"

"No."

It was something embarrassing.

"You were going to explain what happened at the festival," said Wright.

"Smooth change of subject there," Taylan replied. "I like it." She took another piece of candy out of the packet. "Okay, where do I start?"

She told him about the four brothers, Angharad's sons, and their scheme to ruin the Crusader celebration. She told him about her realization, and Marc, and everything that had happened. Some parts she'd only found out later, like the fact that when the time came to trigger the incendiaries, Meilyr and Medwyn had argued, and then fought. Meilyr had wanted to abandon the plan, guessing she and Marc were in danger, while Medwyn had wanted to go ahead with it anyway.

Medwyn had managed to grab the remote detonator and press it.

The final part, after Crusaders had extinguished the flames on her and Marc, was hazy. She'd been too shocked and agonized to register much.

The people had cared for them. Maybe it had been due to Marc's earlier conversation with the Crusader outside the admissions tent, they'd been identified as part of the crowd. She really didn't know. But people had gently cleaned the sticky oil from their burned skin, dressed their wounds, and given them clothes to replace their ruined ones.

Somewhere along the way, the brothers must have noticed what was going on and had claimed Marc as their own. She'd also left the Crusaders soon after, using her damaged airways as an excuse to not speak.

All in all, despite everything that had happened, she was glad she'd done what she had. She only wished she'd managed to persuade Marc to stay away.

She finished her story, and silence fell. The major seemed reluctant to comment on her experiences with the Crusaders.

"I'd prefer to call you Wright, if that's okay."

"You can call me whatever you like. You should bed down for the night. It can't have been easy walking for days with those wounds. Keep the meds. I can do without them. But when Merlin gets back, I want you to let him heal you."

She gave a shiver. "I hate the idea of that creepy alien touching me."

"That's perfectly reasonable. Who wouldn't? But we have a long journey to make to reach the *Gallant*, and you won't be going far or fast in that condition."

She yawned. "Yes, sir."

"A compliant Marine. That's what I like."

"Hey, who said anything about re-enlisting?"

"Just joking. Besides, are you sure the Alliance wants you back?"

"Huh! They'd be lucky to have me."

"They would, and that isn't a joke."

She unrolled her sleeping bag, took off her jacket, and climbed inside, her handmade Crusader clothes feeling awkward and bulky, especially now the major's painkillers were working.

As she settled down, the warmth and happiness she'd felt since encountering Wright began to fade. Patrin and Kayla remained lost and she could never return to the West BI Resistance. If it hadn't been for the mission Merlin had dreamt up, she would have been entirely alone and friendless in a land ruled by someone who wanted her dead.

In truth, she'd had little choice about accepting Wright's proposal.

39

I t was during the journey back to the *Gallant* Wright decided to tell Ellis the information Merlin had revealed. She was wearing one of the suits stowed aboard the dropship in case of emergencies, which meant he could open a one-to-one comm with her and Merlin and Arthur wouldn't overhear.

He knew *she* would believe him. Her opinion of him hadn't been colored by his psych assessment report, as every senior Marine officer's would be from now on. Also, he had a feeling she would have believed him anyway, no matter what any shrink said. She suspected Merlin just as much as he did, and a new level of trust had developed between them.

"So, there are extra-terrestrial powers interfering in Earth affairs," he concluded, "*if* you believe him."

"Whoa." She took a moment to process, then said, "Makes sense. Or, it's some kind of explanation for what's going on. What he's doing here, I mean. Why he's so invested he returned after thousands of years when Arthur woke up. That's a big commitment, right?"

"Who knows what's a big commitment in his terms? He told

me something else that was interesting. I asked him about the alien who accompanies the Dwyr. I said, why aren't we trying to kill her? He replied it would be like trying to kill a rock."

"A rock? She didn't look anything like a rock when I saw her. She did the cloud thing, like he does."

"I suppose it was his way of saying she couldn't be killed. I don't know. It was the usual Merlin obfuscation."

"Do you think the Dwyr's alien is controlling her the way Merlin controls Arthur?" Taylan asked.

"I thought about it, but I've never read any reports about her having a sidekick. She always seemed to be acting alone."

"Maybe her alien returned to Earth the same time as Merlin. Maybe *that's* who snatched the *Fearless*!"

"Yeah," Wright agreed, "you could be right. But why wouldn't he tell us? Why allow suspicion to fall on him?"

"Because he's an asshole who enjoys playing with us."

"You're spot on there."

PREDICTABLY, Colbourn demanded they all reported to her office the moment they set foot on the *Gallant*. Wright led the way, his knee bothering him again. He hoped the higher-ups would allow them some time to recuperate before attempting the assault on the *Belladonna*.

When they arrived, Lieutenant-General Carol was there too. He and the brigadier were standing behind her desk, apparently presenting a united front about something.

"Excellent work, Major," said Carol.

"Thank you, sir."

"No, thank *you* for bringing Corporal Ellis back into the fold."

"Corporal?" said Taylan. "No, I was discharged. I'm just plain Ellis now."

Colbourn coughed. "As I explained when I contacted you a few weeks ago, Major Wright made an error. You are not discharged. Lieutenant-General Carol and I thought we should make that clear so there's no misunderstanding. You still have—"

"No, I'm not a Royal Marine! I only agreed to come back and take part in this mission because Wright asked me. I'm doing you a favor. I am *not* working for you guys anymore!" She stared at Wright accusingly.

"No one told me about this," he said to Colbourn and Carol.

Of course they hadn't told him. He wouldn't have agreed to find her and persuade her to come back if he'd known what they had planned. They probably wanted to control her in the way they couldn't control Arthur or Merlin. They probably saw her as a valuable asset. But they were skating on thin ice. Neither of them understood how much Ellis hated being a Marine.

"The information wasn't relevant at the time," Carol said. "But I thought you understood the discharge you gave was invalid. Your rank doesn't confer the necessary authority. I'm surprised you were unaware of that."

"This is complete rubbish!" Ellis exclaimed. "Fine! I won't do the mission. What are you gonna do? Make me?"

"If you refuse a direct order," Colbourn warned, "you'll be court-martialed."

"Fine. Put me in the brig. I could do with a rest, to be honest. I'm fucking exhausted."

"Do not use that language in front of a senior officer!" barked the brigadier.

"Taylan," Wright interjected, "one of the outcomes of a court martial is execution."

"They could murder me? How bloody dumb is that? Yeah, kill your own personnel. Fantastic idea. It's not surprising the

Alliance is barely holding its own in the war when it has morons like you two running it."

Merlin chuckled.

Colbourn was pale with anger. "You will be silent!"

"Brigadier," said Carol, "if I could say something?" He turned to Ellis. "What do you say we wind back the last few minutes and start again? I can see you feel strongly about the situation. I'll go so far as to say perhaps we underestimated just *how* strongly you would feel. It's an easy mistake to make when we're operating with insufficient information." He glanced at Wright.

Great. Carol expected *him* to shoulder the blame for Ellis's justified outrage.

"Our problem is," the lieutenant-general continued, "we need you and the major here to represent the Alliance in this mission."

"Why?" asked Ellis. "Why can't I be...whatever you count them as." She gestured at Arthur and Merlin.

"Um, that's somewhat difficult to explain," Carol replied. "Suffice to say, at least fifty percent of the core team responsible for the Dwyr's assassination should belong to the Alliance."

It was a political thing, Wright guessed. If it got out that the BA had little or nothing to do with the defeat of the EAC, it would look bad. The Alliance was concerned about its reputation and ongoing influence in world affairs when the war was over.

"Can I suggest something?" he asked.

"Go ahead, Major," said Carol.

"What if you give Ellis a guarantee of her discharge as soon as the mission is over?"

"If I'm still alive," she muttered.

Colbourn gave Carol a look. Her desire to shoot down the possibility was almost palpable.

"I'd have to think about how to organize that within current regulations," Carol replied, "but I'm willing to consider the request."

"Generous of you," said Ellis.

Wright winced.

"Even if you give me a guarantee," she went on, "how am I to know you won't renege on it later? I was given a discharge once, now everyone's backtracking on that."

"If we arrange for a guarantee of some kind, it would be legally binding."

"I could sue you? Come on, it's wartime."

"Believe me," said Carol, "it isn't in our interests to have Marines who don't want to fight."

"It seems the major's identified a potential way forward," Merlin said. "Why don't we all take some time to think about it?"

"That sounds like a splendid idea." Carol clapped his hands together. "You must all be tired after your long journey, *exhausted* even." He smiled at Ellis. "Rest a while, and we'll see what we can come up with."

As they walked away from Colbourn's office, Ellis wouldn't make eye contact with Wright.

"I had no idea they were going to pull that stunt," he said. "As far as I knew, your discharge had gone through."

"Yeah, okay," she replied, but she didn't sound convinced.

40

———

The offer had arrived at Taylan's cabin interface: two lines of text undersigned by Carol *and* the new Chief of Defence Staff. The lieutenant-general had gone to the top, probably in an effort to persuade her. They *really* wanted her to be a Marine, for a short time anyway. If she accepted, her discharge would take effect after the completion of her upcoming assignment.

Along with the proposal came details of her personal file system and security permissions. Pre-empting her acceptance of the terms of the agreement, she'd been added to the *Gallant's* database.

Her files were empty. There was no sign of her vids. They were gone forever.

Turning from the interface on her bedside table, she rolled onto her back. For the first time in her career as a Royal Marine, she had her own cabin.

Carol and Colbourn *really* wanted her for this mission.

And so did Merlin.

No one had explained why.

They'd sent Wright all the way to West BI, making him go

on a long trek through the mountains with Merlin and Arthur to find her—how on Earth they'd managed *that*, she wasn't clear. It had to be something to do with the alien. Then they'd all had to walk to the coast, sail to Ireland, and fly up to the *Gallant*, when all the while some other Marine could have done the job just as well as her, with a lot less wasted time and inconvenience.

What did it mean? Why was she so important? Maybe Wright knew. She should have asked him on their journey, but she'd been too preoccupied with worries and doubts about what she was doing. Maybe she would get an opportunity to ask him later, though she wasn't completely sure she trusted him. He was one of *them*, after all: a Royal Marine, like Colbourn and Carol. She wasn't sure he had her best interests at heart.

No, that wasn't right. She was sure he *didn't*. Before he'd found her, he hadn't known what had gone on since he left her at the Preseli Hills hideout. He would have thought she was still searching for her kids, but he'd come to try to get her anyway.

She'd thought he was a good guy and he was, to an extent, but following orders always came first with him. She would have to be careful to never forget that. She couldn't trust anyone. She would have to look out for herself.

On the other hand, she had the chance to put an end to the long war. If she succeeded in killing the Dwyr, the Britannic Isles would be free again. Things would begin to return to normal, and she might finally find Patrin and Kayla. She wouldn't have to figure out how to survive in a country where she could be shot on sight and even the local Resistance wouldn't have anything to do with her.

In a funny way, it made her happy to think the Crusaders would be free too. Her experience at the midsummer festival had changed her perspective on them. Without a madwoman leading them, filling their heads with superstitions and delusions, they might see how wrong their beliefs were. They might be dragged into modern times.

If the mission failed, she would probably die. If it succeeded, the Alliance wouldn't need her anymore.

What did she have to lose?

She turned onto her side, reached out to the interface, and accepted Carol's offer.

41

———

The *Gallant* had been fitted with massive clamps that would attach to the *Belladonna's* hull when she came alongside the flagship. The problem was, the EAC's vessel was faster than the *Gallant*. When the Alliance Space Fleet troops tried to board her, she could simply pull away and rip off the umbilici. With the clamps in place, wherever she moved, she would take the *Gallant* with her.

It was one of the many new challenges the Alliance strategists had tried to anticipate and pro-actively solve. What the BA was attempting was a first in the history of space warfare. Up until then, boarding only took place when the opponent's ship was crippled. It was the final stage of battle that signaled impending victory. This time, the Space Fleet troops would attempt to board a fully working battleship, all its engines and weapons intact.

The only thing working in their favor was the fact that the *Belladonna* would not be able to deploy any of its heavy armaments. As soon as the attack started, the EAC's other ships would come to the flagship's defense, but with only fifty meters between the *Gallant* and the *Belladonna*, neither would be in a position to target the other. Not only that, destroying another vessel at such close range would inevitably take out the attacker too.

Not that Crusaders were averse to dying in preference to surrender.

The thought brought back painful memories for Wright. He saw again the flash of light as the stadium in Kingston, full of EAC soldiers, exploded, heard the detonation, saw the unmoving bodies of the young men and women he'd been sent to collect.

His orders were to report to the pysch division once the attack on the *Belladonna* was over and undergo therapy. Only when he'd passed an evaluation would he be allowed to return to duty. No one ever stated it out loud, but it was generally accepted that a spell in a psych unit put an end to your military career. There would always be a doubt over your reliability and mettle. At the very least, it would take years to clean the stain from his record and regain his superiors' trust. Most likely, he would never receive another promotion.

"I'm not okay with this," said Ellis. "Are you okay with this?"

She was sitting in a crash seat next to him as the *Gallant* slid silently and invisibly closer to her target.

"Okay with what?" he asked in reply. There were many aspects of the attack that brought him discomfort.

"It doesn't seem right that others have to do the hardest, most dangerous bit while we sit on the sidelines."

Boarding the *Belladonna* would inevitably result in high casualties. The Space Fleet soldiers would be forcing their way through the enemy vessel's airlocks under heavy fire. Consequently, Ellis, Arthur, Merlin, and he were under orders to wait until the ship's defenses were broken through before they began their mission. Their roles were too important to risk their lives in the initial attack.

"Everyone has to play their part," he replied, though he

wondered how old the men and women were who would lose their lives that day. "If we all did exactly what we wanted we'd never win a battle and more lives would be lost."

"If we all did exactly what we wanted," she said, "probably half of us wouldn't even be here."

He couldn't deny the truth of her comment.

"What I don't understand is," she went on, "why they're using the *Gallant* in the attack. I mean, she isn't the biggest ship in the fleet, but she's up there. I know it'll take a lot of troops to fight the *Belladonna's* crew, but wouldn't it make more sense to use dropships? Why risk bringing one of our best battleships next to the EAC's most powerful vessel? If we lose, they'll have another great ship in their fleet."

He explained the problem with the superiority of the *Belladonna's* engines, then also said, "Besides, no dropship is large enough to accommodate the cloaking device. It's massive. The engineers had to remove half the *Gallant's* weaponry and living quarters to fit it. That's why she couldn't take part in the Battle of the *Bres*—the remodeling took a year."

Three minutes to contact, came the general announcement.

He closed his visor.

Nearer the airlocks, the boarding troops waited. When the clamps had engaged, an umbilicus would extend from each airlock and attach to the *Belladonna's*. Sappers would use molecular scalpels to breach the hatches, then the fighting would begin.

Ellis leaned over to touch her helmet to his. "Have you ever seen such a weird couple?" She nodded toward Arthur and Merlin, who sat opposite them on the other side of the passageway.

Arthur had been persuaded to forsake his chainmail and helmet and put on an armored suit, but he hadn't given up his sword. He sat with it propped on the floor, point downward, both his hands resting on the hilt.

Merlin was wearing his attire from the time he'd first appeared in human form: a red robe that extended to his feet and a black cap that covered most of his skull. He'd declined the offer of an EVA suit or any other protection against depressurization.

He had to admit she was right.

Two minutes to contact.

"You know," he said, "I really didn't expect Carol to insist you operate as a Marine for this. If I'd known what he and Colbourn intended, I would have refused to try to find you."

"It's okay. I know how important your job is to you." She moved her helmet away.

She didn't believe him and he didn't know how to convince her.

Patel loomed in his inner vision, and then his last sight of Elphicke.

Fuck.

If Taylan died today, he would never forgive himself.

One minute to contact.

All the small movements of everyone around him ceased. Arthur had his head down. Was he praying? Merlin stared ahead, focusing on nothing.

The seconds ticked away in silence, then, over the comm: *Ten, nine, eight, seven...*

The *Gallant* had been slowing for ages. She came to an abrupt halt, jerking everyone in their seats. The clamps had grabbed the *Belladonna*.

The deck reverberated with the pounding of booted feet as the troops raced to the airlocks. Already, umbilici would be shooting out and latching onto the enemy vessel's hull. The scalpels would be through the thick barrier in no time. Then the hard fight would begin.

Sitting and waiting was agony. All Wright could do was watch his HUD for the signal to move.

A shockwave exploded down the passageway. Somewhere, a grenade had gone off. Was the enemy using them to detach the umbilici? Or were the Alliance throwing them into the *Belladonna* to clear entry to the ship? It was impossible to tell.

His helmet picked up the distant whisper of pulse rifle fire and physical clash of armored bodies.

A Crusader appeared around a corner!

One of them had broken through onto the *Gallant*.

The man ran, confused, glancing over his shoulder, somehow cut off from his fellows.

From his seated position, Wright aimed and fired. The round hit his chest, stopping him in his tracks. He looked down at the hole in his armor.

Meanwhile, Wright had unfastened his harness and was walking toward the hostile. He fired again, hitting the same spot as before. The Crusader fell forward on his face. The body twitched a couple of times before it was still.

His actions had been automatic: see an enemy soldier, shoot to kill.

He'd been doing it most of his adult life. Killing had become second nature to him, he realized.

He seemed to see himself as if from a distance, standing over the dead Crusader.

Then the signal flashed up.

THE *BELLADONNA'S* interior was a hazy, scorched mess. Alliance and EAC troops lay dead in the passageways and fighting continued in other areas of the ship. The vessel was not yet in the BA's hands, but this section was, for now. They couldn't afford to wait until the ship was secured to try to find the Dwyr. The Alliance might be repulsed, so they had to take their chance while they had it.

As ordered, Wright led the search with Ellis, Arthur and Merlin following in their steps.

They moved fast. The *Belladonna* was a huge vessel. If they had to search her top to bottom it would take hours. He guessed the Dwyr would probably be somewhere in the living quarters. She was either in a cabin or the bridge, but he didn't think she would have had time to make it there after the attack began. She would be surrounded by a personal guard by now, no doubt. That was where Arthur would come in.

The deck shook. Somewhere, another grenade had gone off. Smoke puffed down the passageway and streamed into vents as the environmental control tried to clear it. The atmosphere readings on his HUD were going haywire. Somewhere, the ship was depressurizing. Probably multiple places—the clamps piercing her hull, destroyed airlocks, and detached umbilici.

A knot of Crusaders appeared ahead. Ellis fired and Wright joined in. Their pulses splashed over the enemy's suits. One fell. The hostiles moved to fire back, but something made them pause. They were looking past him and Ellis.

After a moment's hesitation, abandoning their fallen comrade, they fled.

Wright glanced back. Arthur was holding his sword aloft.

His formidable presence, along with Merlin's odd garb, must have struck terror into them. The alien's red robes were similar to the Dwyr's ceremonial costumes. They must have been disturbed and confused.

"Major," Merlin said.

"What?"

"This way."

Wright stopped and turned to face the alien. He was pointing at a passageway that branched off the main, heading starboard.

"You can tell where she is?"

"Not her, but someone I believe is with her."

Exasperated, adrenaline making every nerve taut, Wright replied, "Whatever you say."

Ellis's dark visor pivoted toward his, as if questioning his decision. *He* didn't like the idea of Merlin taking over either, but he was anxious to get the job done.

The alien took the new route.

42

Fighting annoyance and reluctance every step of the way, Taylan followed Merlin through the *Belladonna*. Carrying out an assignment on the request of the Britannic Alliance was one thing, doing the alien's bidding was another.

But then, hadn't they been doing his bidding all along, under the guise of fulfilling the BA's aims? He'd been playing them all for fools and she still didn't know exactly why. The story Wright had told her, about Merlin saying he represented powers who supported the Alliance, didn't ring true. Her gut told her his demeanor didn't echo his words.

Nevertheless, she didn't have much of a choice except to trudge along behind him.

Arthur walked alongside the alien, his sword held defensively, while she and Wright regularly checked the rear. The chaotic situation aboard the ship meant threats could come from any angle.

Merlin halted. He seemed to be considering something.

A door slid open and four Crusaders burst into the passageway. She lifted her rifle. Arthur swung around, his sword moved in a wide arc, slicing into a man's bicep and continuing through into his chest. The king heaved the blade out and kicked his victim out of the way. He drove the point into another soldier's stomach, thrusting until the blade emerged from his back.

The remaining two Crusaders leapt backward to get out of his reach, retreating through the doorway. The door slid closed. Two men lay dying in pools of blood, and neither she nor Wright had fired a shot.

Merlin walked on.

She'd been wondering how the king would fare against the Dwyr's troops. The Crusaders he'd killed at the launch ceremony had been mostly unarmed and defenseless. Pulse fire might not affect him, but would he have any effect against suited-up soldiers? Her question had been answered.

Wright opened a one-to-one comm. "I see what you mean about him."

She replied, "You haven't seen anything yet."

"Not far now," said Merlin over his shoulder.

They strode around a corner. Five troops stood abreast, blocking the passageway. More were gathered to their rear.

"This is it," said Wright. "Good luck."

Pulse bolts flew from the enemy's rifles. The energy spilled over Arthur and Merlin...

Merlin was dissolving.

As the Dwyr's female companion at the launch ceremony had, the alien was breaking apart, becoming translucent.

Taylan fired back. Her rounds passed through the space containing the diffusing Merlin. His cloud began to fill the space around her, dark gray and billowing. Trying to ignore the distraction, she marched through it, firing round after round at the enemy. A pulse hit her. Agonizing heat emanated from the spot and she stumbled.

"Behind me, Taylan!" Arthur ordered, taking a long step to get ahead of her.

His arm was up, his elbow pointing back and his sword held tip first as he stamped toward his foes.

These ones did not flee in terror.

She admired their bravery in the face of an attacker unaffected by pulse rounds, but she continued to fire, aiming around Arthur's bulk. Wright's pulses were also flying out.

There could be only one conclusion.

The Crusaders who remained standing by the time they reached them quickly fell to Arthur's sword.

A closed door stood to the right. Behind it, no doubt, was the Dwyr and more of her guard.

Movement at the end of the passageway caught Taylan's attention.

She looked over just in time to see a woman and a boy disappearing around a corner.

It was the Dwyr's companion from the launch ceremony! And the boy had been there too. Rumor said the Dwyr had a son. She guessed that had to be him, and the woman was trying to take him to safety.

Though a surviving successor to Dwyr Orr could mean trouble in days to come, she couldn't help feeling relieved he might get away. She could never have killed him, but she suspected Arthur might have in his berserker rage.

"How do we get in?" she asked Wright.

"There are a couple of possible ways," he replied. "I've let command know we've found her. They can send someone to cut through it, or if we have control of the ship, we can override the security."

Arthur raised his sword.

"Watch out!" she warned Wright.

Arthur plunged it into the security panel. The blade sank in several inches, and the panel sparked and smoked.

"Looks like he can't be electrocuted either," the major remarked. "That won't work," he added, his comm now external. "Breaking the security will seal the door."

The king wrenched the blade free, and then, with a cry, holding the hilt in both hands, he sliced downward.

Taylan's jaw dropped.

The sword had actually pierced the door's surface.

Arthur applied more pressure, forcing the sword in and down. He grunted, his elbows jutting as he worked the blade.

He was cutting through the door!

"Arthur," said Wright, touching the king's elbow.

"Watch out," said Taylan, remembering the scar that remained on her neck from when Arthur had almost killed her.

But the king seemed to hear him.

"Take out your sword and step back," Wright instructed.

She guessed the Alliance must have taken the ship and had told the major they could unlock the door.

Arthur's sword removed, a moment later the door slid open, though only halfway. The ridge the sword had created caught on the jamb.

She was poised, waiting for the defensive fire from within.

Nothing came.

The room was dark.

"Lights," said Wright.

His command had no effect.

Taylan switched her visor to night vision. The room was about four meters square and empty except for a bed. On the bed lay the figure of a woman, curled on her side in a fetal position.

She was slim, and her long, dark hair spread over her pillow.

Was it the Dwyr? For a second, Taylan wondered if they'd been tricked with a decoy. The person on the bed looked very different from the figure she'd seen dressed in all her regalia.

Could it really be her? And what was wrong with her? Why wasn't she getting up? Was she drugged? Could she be dead?

Arthur was striding toward her, his sword high.

"Wait!" Taylan shouted, running in front of him. "Wait! I don't think it's the Dwyr."

This time, he didn't appear to hear.

"Arthur! No!" she pushed his chest, slowing his progress.

She couldn't see his face behind his visor, but she knew the blank stare he was likely wearing too well.

"Wright, help me!" She couldn't let Arthur murder an unarmed woman.

The major didn't move. "It's her."

How did he know? She guessed his HUD had told him, that his helmet was relaying his view of the Dwyr to the *Gallant*.

Arthur raised his sword.

"No! Don't do it!"

In part of Taylan's mind, she saw Dwyr Orr on the platform at the launch ceremony, lifting a knife to Kayla's throat. She saw Wilson, his bloody, tortured body hanging upside down on the front of the Dwyr's conveyance, while the madwoman stood above him behind her protective barrier, the wind billowing out the cloth of her bizarre headdress. She heard the roar of her rabid supporters, clamoring for his blood.

In another part of her mind, Crusaders were tending her burns, giving her their clothes and food. She saw a Crusader couple looking after her son and daughter, knowing they were from West BI and not caring.

There was a sound like air being sucked into a vacuum and suddenly Merlin was there, standing in a corner of the room.

"Don't let him kill her!" she yelled, not even sure why.

The alien said nothing.

She snatched for Arthur's sword arm. At the same time, she kicked his kneecap. It had no effect. She kicked again, summoning all her strength, while barely holding back the descending blade. His armored leg bent backward, just a little, but it was enough to halt his progress.

The king was leaning over her, bringing his considerable weight to bear downward on her. She forced her shoulder into his chest, groaning with effort as she tried to unbalance him. If she could just get him down on the deck, if she could get that sword out of his hand, he might come to his senses.

But what chance did she stand with the alien right there, controlling him?

For long strained seconds, they were at a stalemate. Her hand clamped his wrist and her entire body's power was devoted to preventing the killing blow.

It was not enough.

Her muscles gave way and, the last of her strength spent, she collapsed.

But she fell backward, over the motionless figure of the Dwyr. In another moment, she adjusted her position so she covered the woman's body with her own. She couldn't help it. Everything felt so *wrong*.

Arthur's hand fastened on her shoulder. "Move, Taylan."

"I won't. I can't."

"You must."

His head turned toward Merlin.

Still, the alien said nothing.

Arthur didn't bring down his sword. It hung over her, silver in the dark. But neither did he release her shoulder.

Wright stood by, his rifle muzzle pointing to the side. He also didn't seem to know what to do.

Then Merlin said, "It is no matter. The new leader of the Crusade has escaped on a shuttle. I suggest we take the former Dwyr and return to the *Gallant*."

43

In a remote cove on the coast of West BI, a small boat bobbed on the waves. If it came any closer to the shore, it risked stranding itself on the sea bed. Aboard the boat, an argument was taking place.

"You have to take me closer in," a middle-aged man insisted. "If I try to make it to shore from here, I'll drown."

"I told you," the boat's captain replied, "this is as far as I go. I can't help it that the tide's in, and I'm not going to wait until it goes out. It isn't safe. I've taken a big risk bringing you here."

"I paid you a plentiful amount," said the middle-aged man. "Too much for you to dump me in the sea tens of meters from the coast."

"I'm not dumping you anywhere. I can take you back to Ireland if you like. I'm going that way anyway." The captain grinned.

"No, I don't want to go all the way back to Ireland. I've come this far..." He paused, looking at the waves that lay between him and his destination. "There has to be a better place you can take me."

"Sure, there are lots of spots. I could moor the boat and we could both step onto the quay, right into the hands of Crusader port officials! Now, what's it to be? Are you getting out here, or am I taking you home with me?"

His gaze dropped to the bag hanging from a strap that ran diagonally across the older man's chest. He was clearly wondering what the bag held. Perhaps it was more items similar to the heavy gold necklace he'd accepted in return for passage to West BI.

The man touched his bag protectively and took a step backward.

There was no one else about, naturally. That was the whole idea. He needed to slip into West BI unobserved, especially by anyone from the EAC. But it also meant if a murder were to be committed, there would be no witnesses.

"So, it's back to Ireland it is!" said the captain brightly.

Despite his words, his gaze didn't leave the bag.

"No," said his passenger. "No, I'll get out here." He glanced at the water. How deep was it? He was not a good swimmer. "Perhaps I'll only need to wade in."

"Yes, perhaps. I'll hold that for you while you climb out of the boat and hand it to you once you're in."

"That isn't necessary. I can manage." He moved to the edge. How did one get off a boat at sea? Would he have to jump?

"Are you sure? Your bag looks heavy. It might weigh you down. When you get closer to the shore, I'll throw it to you."

Rather than replying, the man put one leg over the edge of the boat. The gray water churned below him. He paused, trying to gather the courage to put his other leg over.

Too late, he saw the shadow of the captain rushing at him. A grasping hand fastened on the strap across his chest, and the captain tried to yank the bag over his head. The man fought back and managed to land a punch. But he was wobbling, half on and half off the boat. His right leg swung free as the two men tussled.

The captain gave him a shove. He grappled with thin air. He was falling. He felt a tug, and his bag was ripped away, the bulky contents knocking his head as they passed.

Icy water closed over him. He'd taken a breath in shock as he entered it, and the painful, stinging, saltiness filled his mouth and nose. His body rejecting the sensation, the water splurted out, but instantly his lungs reacted with the impulse to breathe in again. He clamped his lips and tried to ignore the spasms that jerked his ribs.

Twisting, flailing, he tried to find the surface. Which way up was he? Where was the sky? He could see nothing. The water was cloudy, opaque. He reached out with his feet but they didn't make contact. Where was the sea bed?

More by luck than effort, his head broke the surface.

Sweet air!

He sucked in a lungful and immediately coughed. He sank below the waves again.

But now he knew in which direction lay his survival.

Inexpertly kicking, he managed to rise to the surface again. His arms windmilled. Was this how to tread water?

His chin and mouth barely visible, he strained to see the boat and caught a glimpse of the stern and the engine chugging away from him.

The damned captain had taken all he had, the wealth he'd spent his entire life collecting. All he had was the clothes he was wearing, a photograph, silver necklace, ceramic pot of fragrant oil, and the coins he'd sewn into his turn ups.

But he had worse problems than few funds.

Where was the shore?

Swinging about, he spotted the beach. It did appear to be deserted, as the captain had promised it would be. He flattened out his body in the water and kicked his legs harder. Tentatively, he moved his arms in a broad breaststroke. That seemed to help keep him afloat, and the waves appeared to be carrying him in the right direction.

The person who had been Hans Jonte slowly swum closer to land.

He had a new name now, one he'd thought up on his long journey from Jamaica: Joseph Fry. What a name to conjure with —memorable, solid, evocative of the old Britannic Isles.

The tip of one of his toes brushed the bottom.

He'd made it.

He put both his feet down and stood up, the cold water streaming from his sodden clothes. A wave crashed into his back, urging him forward. He began to walk the remaining distance to the shingle.

He was going to be okay. He was a survivor.

And though he might have left his old name behind, he hadn't abandoned his dreams, his vision for the future. He would make the right contacts and establish a network. Then, when he was ready, he would begin again.

44

Wright stepped between the opening double doors into bright sunshine. He paused a moment, taking in his surroundings. Palm trees lined the quiet street. The sky was a brilliant blue. It had been a long time since he'd been planetside without being in a combat zone. New Zealand was one of the few remaining places on Earth not currently degraded by resource harvesting or under threat of invasion by the EAC.

His time at the psych unit had done him good. Drug therapies, lots of talking and learning of techniques to help him cope when memories intruded into his mind unbidden. A week seemed too short a time to be there, but he guessed the unit was under pressure to sign off on residents. The Alliance's resources were stretched. Every man and woman was needed.

His orders to return to the *Gallant* had arrived as soon as the doc declared him fit to return to duty. He had a few hours to kill, however, before the transport was due to leave Auckland military spaceport. He decided to take a walk around downtown and maybe buy a few souvenirs of his visit. He'd never bothered with decorating his cabin, but maybe a picture or two would be nice.

He was about to walk away from the unit when someone on the opposite side of the road waved at him.

"Hey, Wright!" she called.

A car approached. After waiting for it to pass, Taylan Ellis crossed the street.

"Phew," she breathed. "I'm glad I caught you. I had to virtually break Colbourn's arm before she would tell me where you were, and then she said I'd miss you because you were leaving today."

He didn't answer. Encountering her here at the unit, knowing she knew he'd stayed for treatment, made him feel weird.

"Is there a bench or somewhere else we can sit?" she asked, then, before he could say anything, she answered her own question. "Yes, there's one. Come on."

The bench stood in a small square of lawn and flower beds to one side of the psych unit entrance, not really large enough to be called a park.

As they sat down, she said, "Hi Taylan. How nice of you to come and see me. How are you?"

He smiled. "Sorry, you've taken me by surprise. But, how *are* you?"

"Better now I can see you're okay. When you disappeared after the battle, I was worried about you."

"Maybe I should have told you where I was going, but I thought you'd be returning planetside at the first opportunity, and...coming here feels a little embarrassing."

"Don't be dumb. It means you're human, unlike Brigadier Bitch Colbourn or Lieutenant-General Carol the Psychopath."

He tried to smother a chuckle, but then gave up smothering it and burst out laughing.

She smiled. "That's good. I think that's the first time I've heard you laugh properly."

"Have you been aboard the *Gallant* all this time?" he asked.

"I have. I received my official discharge, then I kind of hung around under the radar. Things were crazy after we took the Dwyr to the *Gallant*, right? I think the Alliance could barely believe its luck. No one was paying any attention to me so I took the time to sort out some stuff."

"What's been happening?" One of the standard rules of treatment at the unit was no access to news.

"Hmm, did you know Ua Talman announced he's lending his support to the Alliance?"

"I didn't. That's great. We might win this war yet. Did he say what was behind his decision?"

"I don't think he did. Or I didn't hear about anyway. Oh, *and*," she said added in the tone of someone about to impart some juicy gossip, "the word is, Dwyr Orr is in a coma. That's why she was so unresponsive when we found her. The docs can't bring her out of it."

"Really?"

"Yes. In fact, I know it's true because Arthur told me."

"You're friends with him again?"

"Not exactly. I mean, he's come close to killing me twice now, so...you know? But he did seem to want to make it up to me somehow. It's odd. Deep down, he's extremely moral as well as kind and well-meaning. On the other hand, he's also a blood-thirsty, remorseless killer."

"But he's only ever like that when Merlin's around," said Wright.

"Yes, something comes over him, and he does the alien's bidding. I'm not certain, but I think the fact that I tried to stop him both times might have made him think twice about Merlin."

"That's good news. And what's happening with the EAC?"

"It's going just as strong as ever. It announced it has a new leader, Dwyr Perran Orr."

"The boy."

"Yes, Kala's son," Taylan agreed. "But we all know he's too young to lead. The real leader is that woman who escaped with him."

"I said something similar to Merlin once. I suggested she might be our real enemy, that *she'd* encouraged the original Dwyr in her ambition to convert the entire globe to her cult."

"What did he say?"

"He said..." Wright scrunched his brow as he tried to remember. "He complimented my insight. That was all, though."

"He did?! Then maybe you're right. Maybe he was saying you hit the nail on the head."

"Maybe, but what good will it do us? He also said she's impossible to kill."

Taylan also frowned. Then she appeared to become distracted by something. She was staring at a spot around the top of his head.

She reached out a tentative hand and gently pressed the crown of his hair. "Doesn't it ever stay down?"

She was referring to the irrepressible tuft.

"Never," he replied. "But, one day, everyone will wear their hair like this."

She snorted with laughter. "I expect you're right. When mine grows back..." she self-consciously touched the short regrowth on one side of her head "...I'm getting it cut just like yours."

A plaintive miaow came from the bag at her feet. "Oh, I almost forgot! Poor Boots. He's been cooped up in there for ages."

"You brought the ship's cat to Earth with you?"

"He was never the ship's cat. He was always *my* cat. I left him on the *Fearless* because I couldn't look after him in West BI, but I got Abacha to have him transferred to the *Gallant*, and now he's yours. You *will* take good care of him, won't you?"

"I...er..."

"He's very cuddly when he gets to know you, and he's trying really hard to be house-trained."

Wright thought of his sparse cabin. "I'd be honored."

Taylan grinned. "I knew you would say yes."

She quickly became serious again. "You know what Abacha said once when we were playing xiangqi? He said we were like the pieces on the game board, to be defeated and discarded by the people playing the game. *They* never come to any harm, only us poor pieces. That's how I feel about Merlin and the other alien who's now controlling the EAC. They can't be hurt, but they'll happily see us die to achieve their aims."

"What are their aims, I wonder?" Wright asked.

"I don't know, and I don't know how to find out." She heaved a sigh.

"What are you going to do now?"

"What else can I do? I have to go back to West BI. But I have a new idea to follow up, a different approach to take. I hope I'm right this time."

"I hope so too, Taylan."

"Thank you." She stood up. "I have to catch a flight to Ireland. Take care, Major T.J. Wright."

She bent down to kiss his cheek before leaving.

Taylan and Wright's story continues in

THE RESOLUTE

(Amazon.com link. For your country's Amazon, scroll to the
end of the book.)

AUTHOR'S NOTES

Hello and welcome to the juicy tidbits of extra information at the end of the book. Many thanks for sticking with me thus far in the telling of the Star Legend, and thanks once more to my awesome shipmates, especially Liza Wood, Mike Phillips, Mike Paddick, and the Review Crew, who have all helped to make the series possible.

When I was deciding what to include here I considered mentioning Lagrange Points, protocells, the block universe theory (Morgan's explanation for her view that time doesn't exist), and other nerdy stuff mentioned in *The Gallant*. But you're a science fiction reader and you already know about that kind of thing, right? Instead, here are some equally interesting items to ponder.

Ynys Mon and Bryn Celli Ddu

Ynys Mon is the Welsh name for Anglesey, an island close to the north-west coast of Wales. If you love disappearing down rabbit holes and have a spare few months, I recommend reading up on Ynys Mon's long and fascinating history. Associated from antiquity with druids, the island is rich in prehistoric sites, including Bryn Celli Ddu, which means "the mound in the dark grove". This ancient passage tomb where the Crusaders hold their midsummer festival dates back to 4000 BC. In an excavation of the site, archaeologists found cremated human remains at the bases of some of the henge stones, and a single human ear bone was found under a flat slab. That's right, a single human ear bone.

Meilyr and His Brothers

Fans of Arthurian legend have probably already guessed who Meilyr and his three brothers are based upon. If you don't know, don't worry as it doesn't impact the story. However, if you think you know, I can confirm, yes, it's *those* four brothers. If you want a clue, I am really looking forward to the release of the film *The Green Knight* later this year (2021).

The Yew Circle

The circle of yews surrounding the ruined chapel that Arthur wanted to visit was inspired by Llanfengan Yew Circle, possibly a remnant of a pre-Christian site. Yews were sacred to druids and Celts associated them with death, maybe due to the toxicity of their needles. This association continued into the Christian era, resulting in the tree being regularly planted in churchyards. For more information read Janis Fry's books, one of which is called *Warriors at the Edge of Time*—as fine a name for a book as anyone could imagine.

Arthur's Worldview

One of the most challenging aspects of fiction writing is to stay true to a character's perspective of the world and their place within it. King Arthur is supposed to have lived around the fifth or sixth century, which makes portraying his world-view even harder. I have tried to incorporate into his point of view both his deep religiosity and his intimate association with nature, rather than being separated from it as most modern humans are. My understanding is derived from years of interest and research in this area, so it's hard to recommend a single resource for more information, but you could start with Tristan Gooley's *The Natural Navigator*.

If you'd like to read Star Legend book four, *The Resolute*, a few weeks earlier than it will appear on Amazon, become a Patreon supporter.

To chat about the series or meet other readers, come along to the Starship JJ Green Shipmates Facebook group. I'd love to see you there.

Sign up to my reader group for exclusive free books, discounts on new releases, review crew invitations and other interesting stuff:

https://jjgreenauthor.com/free-books/

DOWNLOAD YOUR FREE READERS' GUIDE TO THE SCIENCE FICTION NOVELS OF J.J. GREEN

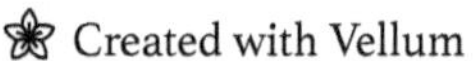 Created with Vellum